Give Me Thine

Heart

Also by Andrea Boeshaar

····ᘜ❤ᘞ····

MY HEART BELONGS…
in the Shenandoah Valley: Lily's Dilemma[#]

SHENANDOAH VALLEY SAGA
A Thousand Shall Fall: A Civil War Novel[*]
Too Deep for Words: A Civil War Novel[*]
There is a Season: A Civil War Novel (July 2019)[†]

FABRIC OF TIME SERIES
Threads of Hope[‡]
Threads of Faith[‡]
Threads of Love[‡]

[#] Barbour Publishing
[*] Kregel Publications
[†] Steeple View Publishing LLC
[‡] Charisma House

Give Me Thine Heart

ANDREA BOESHAAR

Steeple View Publishing, LLC

Cover Design & Interior Formatting: Crystal L Barnes
http://www.booksbybarnes.com

Model Photograph by Period Images
https://www.periodimages.com/

Editorial Review: Spit 'n' Polish Editing
Ellen Tarver, Editor

Published by Steeple View Publishing LLC
P. O. Box 33
Newburg, WI 53060
SteepleViewBooks@gmail.com

Printed in the United States of America.

All Scripture is taken from the King James Version of the Holy Bible.

Dedication

No professional author is the end all and be all of any book project. I'm certainly not. There are critique partners, editors, cover designers, proof readers, and formatters who are involved. So this story is dedicated to all those wonderful individuals I've got on my publishing team who encouraged and assisted me with this endeavor.

May Jesus Christ be praised!

Scripture

My son, give me thine heart, and let thine eyes
observe my ways.

Proverbs 23:26

Chapter One

Kingsley Manor
Periwick, England
July, 1814

Ladies in pastel gowns of pink, green, and blue skipped by as the orchestra played a lively tune. Then, forming a long row, the ladies danced in a circle across from their dashing male counterparts, also in a line. The men made the same circular motion followed by claps and hoots.

"Hey!" they shouted in unison in time with the music.

Moira Kingsley peeked around one of the enormous pillars in Uncle Tyrus's ballroom and fought back the overwhelming feeling that she was terribly out of her league. Never had she been to such a festival—and she, the honored guest. What a relief that she could stand in the shadows where no one noticed her.

She stifled a yawn and supposed she ought to appear somewhat enthusiastic. After all, this was her engagement party.

Standing to her full height of five feet seven inches— gigantic by fashionable standards—she tried to remember the straight posture that Aunt Aggie taught her. But unless she hunched just a little, she could look down on most men, Uncle Tyrus included. Aunt Aggie said Moira's stature caused men to feel uncomfortable and, therefore, she ought to be grateful that Major Joseph Nettles agreed to wed her.

Moira's gaze slowly slid to the man to whom she'd recently become betrothed. Somehow it had occurred without her even being present. No long looks and courtship. No conversation and promises. Just the engagement.

A shudder ran through her. As an officer of His Majesty's Royal Army, the major did make a formidable figure in his uniform of white breeches, tunic, and red coat with its impressive gold shoulder boards. However, he also made Moira's skin crawl despite his reputation of having a way with the ladies. Even now he stood boasting while three eyelash-batting females hung on his every word. But Moira wasn't envious. The sight only evoked apathy…and dread.

Truth to tell, she wasn't fond of the man and had no delusions about their impending nuptials. Nettles would not be a loving, faithful husband. Very simply, he was marrying her for her inheritance, nothing more.

The dance ended and applause broke out for the orchestra. Couples dispersed. Men fetched cups of fruity punch for their partners as well as for themselves. Moira counted two people she knew fairly well in the room—her aunt and uncle. The rest were their neighbors and friends, and people she'd met only in passing.

If only Mum and Papa were here…

An ache in her chest began to grow, just as it did each time she recalled her parents and that horrible night in a Uganda village not even a year ago. Uncle Tyrus said her life as a missionary was dead and gone. Like Mum and Papa. Why, then, could she not let go of the past? Instead, in her mind's eye, she saw flames reaching high into the starry sky. She heard the piercing screams of the tortured and dying. She recalled Papa's last words to her, "Hide in the rushes by the riverbank." He'd pulled the silver cross and chain from around his neck and pressed it into her palm. "Stay there. Not a peep..."

Moira fingered the treasure she now constantly wore, the cross resting close to her heart. She'd never forget. Never!

"Miss Kingsley?"

Startled from her muse, she lifted her gaze. Two men stared at her. One older fellow, familiar to her, wearing a curious expression, powdered wig, gold silk waistcoat, and black tailcoat. The younger man, whose piercing blue eyes seemed to hold her captive, looked like a fine figure to be sure, judging from the way his broad shoulders filled his tailcoat. His muscular upper arms seemed to stretch the fabric to its limits. His sandy-brown hair looked kissed by the sun and was combed neatly back and secured in a queue with a simple black ribbon.

Best of all, the man stood taller than she by at least four inches.

"Miss Moira Kingsley—" The rich tone of the older man's voice pulled her from her thoughts. "I'd like to introduce one of my esteemed students. Mr. Samuel White."

"Miss Kingsley..." The younger of the two gave her a polite bow.

"A pleasure, I'm sure." She pushed out a smile, as her cheeks warmed. She'd been ogling the poor fellow. How utterly embarrassing!

By grace alone, Moira recalled the older man's name. Sir Nathaniel Potter, a professor at the university and one of Uncle Tyrus's good friends.

"My dear, are you well?" Sir Nathaniel's furry gray brows met over the bridge of his bulbous nose. "You look a bit peaked."

"I'm quite all right, Sir Nathaniel. Thank you. Perhaps it's all the excitement."

"Ah, of course." The older gent puffed out his chest and smiled. "Your uncle found a fine catch for you." He spoke as she if were a John Dory snagged by an expert fisherman.

Nausea wafted upward from the pit of her gut.

"Moira." Her name sounded somewhat majestic, rolling off Mr. White's tongue. "Your name means destiny or fate."

"Does it now?" She tipped her head, feeling mildly intrigued. "I never knew that."

"Yes, which means, of course, that I must ask the bride-to-be to dance." Mr. White smiled and gave another bow.

"Dance? Me?" Finally for the first time tonight, someone chose to pay her a bit of attention. "Why?"

Mr. White grinned, revealing a set of strong, even teeth. He arched a charming brow. "I make a habit of dancing with only the prettiest ladies at the parties I attend."

"I'm sure you do," Moira retorted.

Sir Nathaniel snorted a laugh and clapped Mr. White between the shoulder blades.

Moira found Mr. White amusing as well. "You may ask me then, sir." Whether a gentleman or knave, she'd make him work for the honor.

"Miss Kingsley," he began with an earnest expression, "will you dance with me?"

"I will."

His features lit up and he offered his gloved hand.

Moira took it and he led her to where the other dancers were getting into place.

"The bride-to-be must call the dance!" Mr. White shouted above the din.

All eyes shifted to Moira. Her lips moved, but her mind went blank. She didn't dare disgrace her aunt and uncle by blurting out something inappropriate.

Mr. White bent his head as if listening to words which never quite formed on her tongue. "The lady calls for a French waltz."

Moira froze in utter horror while gasps and whispers filled the room. No other dance could be more controversial. In fact, many people deemed the waltz quite scandalous.

"A French waltz it is." The lead musician appeared quite gleeful about it.

Several couples walked away in a huff while others quickly took their places on the dance floor.

A young lady beside Moira clapped her gloved hands with excitement. "An excellent choice, Miss Kingsley."

"I'm glad you think so." The muscles in Moira's shoulders began to unwind as she glimpsed other happy expressions from the younger crowd. It seemed a suitable dance after all.

The music began to play and Mr. White opened his arms.

She watched the lady beside her, then copied the move and found herself in Mr. White's embrace. "I shall admit, sir, that I am not well practiced with this new dance."

"Not to worry, Miss Kingsley. Simply follow my lead."

Something about the way he spoke sounded foreign on Moira's ears. She back stepped and Mr. White directed her in a slow pirouette.

"Are you an American?"

His blue eyes twinkled. "Will you give me away if I say that I am?"

"Surely not." In his arms once more, she added, "I care

nothing about this war with the colonies."

"But your fiancé could be killed."

Dared she hope? "His Maker's choice, not mine."

Mr. White gracefully swept her across the polished wooden floor, keeping time with the other couples.

Moira caught the scowl on Uncle Tyrus's face as she whirled passed him. Perhaps this wasn't such a good idea…

She took in Mr. White's uplifted features, his charming smile, and, oddly, Uncle Tyrus's deep frown vanished from her thoughts.

She then caught sight of Major Nettles holding in his arms one of the women with whom he'd been conversing earlier. He held her much closer to himself than society dictated—even for a French waltz. Could that have been the reason for Uncle's displeasure?

Most likely yes.

The last of Moira's misgivings dissipated and she gave her full attention to her partner. She smiled as he led her in a broad circle while twirling around the room. She heard "oohs" and "ahhs" from onlookers and it added to her growing pleasure.

Mr. White gave her an unexpected spin and Moira giggled. Stepping in close to him again, she heard the rumble of laughter in his chest.

"Are you having fun, Miss Kingsley?"

"The time of my life, Mr. White."

He spun her around again, taking her by surprise once more. Moira felt lighter than air and hardly the gargantuan Aunt Aggie made her out to be.

"So charm is not your only attribute." She felt slightly breathless. "You're an expert dance partner too."

"You flatter me, Miss Kingsley."

Moira knew of his ilk, a man quite accustomed to female

compliments and companionship. Still, she enjoyed his attention.

They made another round of the room, the ornately plastered walls a pleasurable blur. When they neared the opened portico doors again, Mr. White stopped and politely led her outside.

"A breath of air?"

"Yes, I quite need it. Thank you." Her face flamed from unaccustomed exertion. While living in the Uganda village with her parents, she had been physically active all day. She and Mum taught children at school and frequently Moira played with them. She'd imagine all sorts of games, and the children adored her because she made them smile and laugh. But here in Periwick, she'd been rendered virtually useless and did far too much sitting, both indoors and out.

Oh, how she missed the life she'd lived with Mum and Papa...

"Miss Kingsley? Did you hear what I asked?"

She snapped from her reverie and heaved a sigh laden with guilt. "Nay, I'm afraid my mind wandered." She focused on the handsome Mr. White. "Forgive me. What did you say?"

"A stroll in the gardens?"

She smiled. "I'd like that. Thank you."

Moira took his arm and they headed for Auntie's pride and joy—her blooms. As they walked deeper into the darkness, the music and laughter from the house grew distant. Moira realized her folly and stopped short. She knew nothing of this man. To go farther might mean her screams would not be heard, should he try to take advantage of her.

And yet, she felt safe enough.

"May I be frank, Miss Kingsley?"

"Of course."

Mr. White cleared his throat. "I daresay I have never seen a more unhappy bride-to-be."

"Is it that obvious?" Moira gazed upward at the sparkling stars. "I should be more grateful, I suppose."

"Should you?"

"Of course. Joseph Nettles is an officer and an upstanding man…or so I hear." Moira shifted uncomfortably and stared into Mr. White's shadowed face. She had never strolled in the gardens with Major Nettles. The man largely ignored her when he visited Uncle Tyrus, although discussions of war machines and battles seemed to animate him.

But if Papa were here things would be different. Papa would dislike Nettles for his narrow view of humanity. Of that Moira felt certain. The major would rather kill his enemy than show him God's love.

She bent to inhale the delicate fragrance of Auntie's roses.

"Major Nettles is fortunate to be marrying such a lovely young lady as yourself. Why, you rival these blossoms."

"Ah, but you have not seen them in daylight." Moira smiled. "Nonetheless, I thank you for the compliment. However, I know what I am. I'm as plain and ordinary as that patch of daisies there." She pointed behind the fore-flowers. "I'm filler. Nothing special."

"You are speaking of the feverfew, otherwise known as the daisies to which you referred." He inclined his head. "The American natives consider feverfew quite valuable. It's lovely, hearty, and has strong medicinal properties."

"Do they now?"

"Indeed."

She narrowed her gaze. "You're teasing me?"

"Surely not!"

Moira put her gloved fingers against her lips and

swallowed a laugh. In truth, she enjoyed needling him, scholar that he was said to be. "Tell me more of American natives."

"Well, I must confess, I'm mostly familiar with the Catawba of South Carolina." Beneath the stream of moonlight, Moira admired his strong profile and proud set of his jaw. "They're a brave people who fought with Americans during the Revolutionary War and now the Second War of Independence from England." He leaned toward her rather conspiratorially. "Not good news for your Major Nettles, I'm afraid."

"He does not belong to me. Alas, I doubt he ever will." Not that she harbored such a hope. "He belongs to the battlefield, I'm afraid."

"Moira!" The object of her statement hailed her from the edge of the garden. Within moments he reached them. The brass buttons of his red coat glimmered beneath the moonlight. "What are you doing out here? And without a shawl!"

"I needed a breath of air, 'tis all, and it's a balmy night; I'm warm enough." She indicated her escort. "Please meet Mr. Samuel White. Mr. White, allow me to present Major Joseph Nettles."

"Yes, yes, we've met." Nettles impatiently waved off the introduction. To Mr. White, he said, "I'm headed to Baron Kingsley's study for a smoke. Care to join me? You'll meet others in His Majesty's Royal Army. Perhaps you'll even join our endeavors to crush the Americans." He fisted the air as if such a conquest lay within his grasp.

Moira didn't breathe.

"Thank you. I'll be along shortly." Mr. White's voice sounded assured despite the threat of a crushing. He was an American, after all.

But perhaps the man sided with the British. Many did…

Nettles hesitated and glanced between Mr. White and Moira.

She looked away, toward Auntie's flower garden, although she'd done nothing of which to be ashamed. Still she felt a strain—as though something wasn't quite right.

"I'll see Miss Kingsley back to the house."

"She knows the way," Nettles grumbled.

Moira faced Mr. White while inexplicable hurt spiraled down inside of her. Perhaps she'd delighted in this man's attention a few moments too long. Perhaps she wished she was marrying a man who cared about her—who loved her.

"Major Nettles is correct. I need no escorting."

"See? Now, come on, man." Nettles attempted to propel Mr. White by the upper arm.

He pulled free and didn't budge. "I said, I'll be along shortly." His voice beheld an edge sharper than any saber.

A moment of tension passed between the two men and Moira noticed that Mr. White stood a good two inches taller than the major. Indeed, from her vantage point Nettles appeared dwarfed in Mr. White's shadow.

At last Nettles gave a shrug. "As you wish."

Moira watched her intended's retreating back as he marched, rather than walked, back to the house. She suddenly envisioned a home run like a military academy, children marching in a row, sitting, eating, reading, writing, all at the commander's will. And what would become of her? Would she be transformed into a wooden-headed doll, poised in every manner which her possessor wished, as though she had no mind of her own?

"Oh, that I had wings like a dove!" Moira closed her eyes, praying it might be so. "For then would I fly away, and be at rest."

"Ah, you quote the Psalms." Mr. White's tone returned to its honeyed charm. "Quite comforting in turbulent times, are they not?"

"They are." Moira pressed her lips together. She oughtn't to have spoken the passage aloud. "Please forgive me. I hear many brides-to-be struggle with anxiety. That's all this is. Prenuptial nerves." She rubbed her bare arms. "And why I am speaking to you of this, I don't know."

Mr. White shrugged out of his frockcoat and placed it around Moira's shoulders. It smelled of him, a leathery, woodsy spicy scent that she found not at all unpleasant.

"Never fear, Miss Kingsley." He offered his arm. "I'm a superb secret-keeper."

"What a relief, for I am the luckiest young lady in all of England."

The words already felt mechanical. It was with much trepidation that she allowed herself to be escorted back to her uncle's house.

17

Chapter Two

From his vantage point near the entryway of Baron Kingsley's smoky study, Sam could see the lovely, but quite miserable, bride-to-be standing a ways off from the mingling crowd. How he pitied her and wished he could help her somehow. But he had a sworn duty, and by God, he'd use all his wits to see the job through.

He turned his attention to the British officer speaking. Most of the men, including him, had shed their tailcoats while they enjoyed their pipes.

"Those uncouth colonists thought they could steal Canada right out from under us." The officer snorted with obvious derision. "But we'll show them. We've set our sights on the U.S. Capital!"

The room erupted in a roar as cheers went up.

"And just how do you plan to do this deed?" Uncrossing his arms, Sam strode farther into the room. "I've heard the American militiamen are fierce."

Laughter met his last statement.

"My dear, naïve friend," Major Nettles began, "you have much to learn. Then again, you are a student, are you not?"

"I am." The perfect disguise.

"Then learn from the best." Nettles indicated the surrounding officers. "The American militia cannot possibly stand against His Majesty's armed forces! Why, nothing is left of the American Navy. They use merchant vessels and have no gunboats. American militiamen are unskilled and untrained in the practices of war." He set his jaw. "We will soon take back the colonies for the crown."

More cheers.

A smile tugged at the corner of Sam's mouth as he waited for the room to quiet. "And what of the First Nations?"

"The Indians? Bah! They are savages." Nettles shrugged. "Although some fight for the Crown. So what of them?"

"Others fight with the Americans. Do you not fear them— fear being captured and tortured by them?"

"Tsk, tsk, tsk…" Nettles wagged his head facetiously. "Dear boy, a British soldier, one worthy of his shoulder boards, has no fear."

"Not even of losing his scalp?"

"Not even that." A sneer wafted across Nettles's pronounced features. "Anymore questions…*boy*?"

Sam grinned. He would not be goaded.

"Perhaps it's time you become a man," another soldier injected. "Sign up for His Majesty's Royal Army."

"I shall consider it." *On my first day in hell*. A chuckle escaped. By God's grace, Sam had little fear of either fate.

Sam headed toward the rum and poured himself a small glass.

"So tell me, how long before British officers attack the American capital? Should we board a ship and sail tomorrow, would we make it in time to join the fray?"

"Doubtful, my scholarly friend." Nettles puffed on his

pipe. "We're leaving the details to General Robert Ross and his forces. It shall be payback for the American attack on the City of York." A muscle in the man's jaw worked. "I lost someone I loved very much in that battle. A bloody mess is what it was."

"You speak as if you know of it firsthand?"

"I do." Nettles's dark gaze attempted to spear Sam. "I wasn't far away, on duty in Ontario. Our troops arrived, only too late. The Americans tortured and raped women before killing them in front of their children. A few survived to tell of the massacre."

"Appalling." Sam recalled the event a bit differently. Yes, the citizens of York had been frightened from their sleep, and Sam eschewed violence against innocents. But, truth to tell, British troops accosted American civilians more often than militiamen harassed Canadians.

"Appalling indeed." Nettles lifted his chin. "And mark my words, the Americans will suffer for it. General Ross will see to it."

Growls of agreement filled the study.

Sam digested the information and downed his rum before setting aside the glass. He took his place near the entrance once more. He would take his leave shortly, but not too soon to arouse suspicion. He'd learned that General Ross must be stopped and the U.S. Capital reinforced. He needed to get that piece of information, as well as others, to President Madison in time.

However, to do so he had to be on the ship tonight before it set sail for America.

Sam glanced across the way and stood to his full height, every nerve drawn tight, sending prickles of warning down the back of his neck. There, in the receiving parlor where all the smokers had shed their tailcoats stood Miss Kingsley—

And in her hands lay Sam's black diary, containing news that was not for her eyes!

He slipped from the room and crossed the large foyer. As he approached, she looked up and smiled when she saw him. Her smoky-gray eyes held only a welcome, no fear or guilt from being caught snooping.

"What have you got there, Miss Kingsley?"

She glanced to the black book in her long, slender hands. "I don't know. I found it on the floor." She leafed through it. "Evidently it fell out of someone's coat pocket."

"So you took it upon yourself to read it?" Sam didn't attempt to curb his sharp tone. Most likely she intended to run to her fiancé with what she learned.

"I read only enough to find out the book's owner, is all." Miss Kingsley tipped her head and strands of her straw-colored hair slipped from its pins. They fanned her cheek. "Does it belong to you?"

In reply, Sam held out his hand.

"I thought maybe it did." She handed it over.

Sam bent to collect his tailcoat. From the way it lay in the pile, he could see how his diary had slipped from its hold. Perhaps Miss Kingsley had found it on the floor, but now she put him in a precarious position. He couldn't take the chance of being discovered. Not now.

"Blast it all!" he snarled.

"Excuse me?"

Sam pulled on his coat and sheathed his diary. He buttoned the coat up the front, his gaze never wavering from her lovely face.

"I assure you, Mr. White, much of what I read made no sense, and that which I did understand I shall keep to myself.

You have my word."

Her promise meant nothing to him at this moment. In one swooping motion, he took hold of the knife he kept hidden inside his left boot and slapped his palm over her mouth to prevent a scream. "Miss Kingsley, I'm afraid I must kill you."

No fear entered her eyes. She merely nodded and peeled away his fingers. "Are you a spy?" Her whispered breath touched his cheek.

Sam wasn't about to answer the question. He pushed her farther into the room.

"I would suggest killing me in that corner there." She pointed toward a narrow alcove. "You can stuff my lifeless body beneath the writing desk. No one will even notice I'm gone…until, of course, the stench is overpowering."

"Do you think this is a game?" One hand on her upper arm, Sam gave her a shake. "Do you think I'm playing here? I promise you, Miss Kingsley," he sneered, "I am not!"

"I know. I can tell." She still kept her voice low. "But might I ask, Mr. White, that you make it quick? I'm not afraid to die. I simply don't want it to hurt."

Sam caught the pleading light in her gray eyes. "You're joking?"

"I'm not. Death is preferable to life as Major Nettles's wife." A faraway look entered her gaze. "In death I shall be reunited with my beloved parents and all the souls to whom we've had the privilege to minister." Her eyelids fluttered closed. She inhaled deeply. "I'm ready."

Holding the knife's sharp blade near her throat, Sam found he couldn't do the deed. Oddly, killing a woman who had no fear of death and one who actually wanted to die seemed to defeat the purpose.

Besides, he'd never killed anyone other than in self-defense. And never a woman!

Miss Kingsley peeked at him through one opened eye. "Hurry and do it before you're discovered."

Sam shoved the knife back into his boot, noting the obvious surprise then disappointment that wafted across her pretty features.

She stood wide-eyed now. "You're not going to kill me?"

"No." Sam released the breath he hadn't been aware he'd been holding. "Count yourself lucky."

"I don't believe in luck."

"Blessed, then." Had she said her father was a minister?

"Cursed, is more like it." Her shoulders sank forward. "I've been pleading with the Lord to intervene in this fate worse than death called an engagement. I thought, by your murdering me, Jesus meant to take me to my heavenly home."

"I trust you'll forget anything you read and keep your mouth shut, or I shall have to reconsider."

She said nothing, her gaze fixed on his face.

Prickles of guilt inched their way to Sam's heart. Miss Kingsley's misery was palpable. He exhaled audibly.

"On second thought..."

She cocked her head and regarded him.

"I shall take you with me."

She snapped to attention. "To the colonies?"

"Shh!" Sam held his forefinger against his lips.

"To America?" she whispered this time. She took two steps toward him. "May I be a spy like you? I'd be a very good one. People say all manner of things around me because they don't realize I'm paying attention—or that I'm even in the room."

Sam worked the threatening smile off his lips. "How fast can you pack a valise?"

"In minutes. I own very little."

Odd. Baron Kingsley was a wealthy man. Well, no matter…

"Gather your belongings in one bag—and only one. Do not let anyone see you. Meet me out in back by the carriages in ten minutes. If you're caught, stash the bag and get yourself outside."

She gave a nod to each command. "I'll get right to it."

Sam grabbed her upper arm as she attempted to pass. He gripped her harder than necessary…just in case she got the notion to turn on him. "Say nothing to no one or I'll toss you into the sea. Do you understand?"

Finally a flicker of fear. "I understand." She pressed her coral-pink lips together and the wayward thought of kissing her scampered across Sam's brain.

Madness. Sheer madness! Had he been smart, he'd have killed her.

He let her go and she scurried from the room.

He kneaded his jaw and forced his mind back to reality. How in the world could he use this situation to his advantage and for his cause?

Chapter Three

.... ᠺ♥ᠹ ....

Moira silently slipped into her bedchamber. A lamp flickered on the small table beside the bed. Her lady's maid jumped up from the rocking chair and curtsyed.

"You may go, Betsy. I believe the rest of the household staff is enjoying some sweet treats in the kitchen. I shall call if I need you. Right now I wish to have some time to myself."

The dark-haired maid replied with another dip. "Yes, ma'am." She left the room.

Moira turned the lock on the door and quickly moved to the high wardrobe at the other end of the room. She found her tapestry-covered valise, set it on her bed, and pulled it open. Gathering her underthings from her wardrobe drawers, she stuffed them into the mouth of the hungry bag. Next she slipped a couple of her frocks from their hangers, rolled them up, then stuffed them into the valise. She packed a few special trinkets and, of course, her Bible, recalling the last time she was forced to pack quickly.

She'd been only ten years old, some eight years ago. Her parents received the notice from their church's Missions Board: they would go to Uganda and minister to the villagers there.

But this was not ministry. This was escape.

Moira paused to consider her impending actions. Could she trust Mr. White? Did it matter? She'd welcome death, so any life had to be better than marriage to Major Nettles! Besides, Moira saw something in Mr. White's azure gaze, a spark of candidness, so rare these days, and it won both her respect and trust.

Moira packed the rest of her belongings, making sure to take her stockings, her warmest wrap, and sturdy leather everyday booties which properly covered her ankles. Then, tying on a wide-brimmed hat and with a lighter shawl around her shoulders, her best slippers still on her feet, she quietly made her way down the servants' stairwell in the back of her uncle's manor. She could hear laughing wafting up from the kitchen. It was almost too easy. Within seconds, she was outside where carriages lined the drive.

The crisp *snap-snap* of two fingers claimed Moira's attention. She stared in the direction from which they'd come. Mr. White stepped out of the shadows, took up her valise in one hand and clasped her elbow with the other.

"This way," he whispered.

She followed him as they slipped in and around the parked carriages until they reached one that appeared to be a hired hackney coach. After tossing her bag up to the driver, Sam opened the door and helped Moira inside. He mumbled something to the driver before climbing in and closing the door. He sat on the bench beside her. Her bare forearm rubbed against the fabric of his frockcoat.

"We're going around to the front to pick up Sir Nathaniel, so you might want to think up some tale as to why you're sharing our hired hack this evening." Mr. White leaned forward. "Since you asked to be a spy, consider this a test to prove your worthiness of the role."

Moira lifted her chin. "I shan't disappoint you." She rummaged through her mind, back over the volumes she'd read recently—Shakespeare, Henry Fielding, Maria Edgeworth, Fanny Burney, and Daniel Defoe. What would the pirate Captain Singleton do in such a situation?

By the time Sir Nathaniel strutted to the coach, she'd decided the less she said the better.

The professor climbed inside. "Why, Miss Kingsley," he declared as he sat opposite her and Mr. White. "What on earth are you doing in here?"

"Shh…" She placed a gloved finger against her lips. "It's a surprise for Major Nettles."

"A surprise?" Several moments of laden silence lapsed. Moira held her breath. At last, Sir Nathaniel broke into laughter. "A surprise! Of course. Oh, my dear girl, I just adore surprises."

The coachman closed the door and, with a slight jerk, they were off.

She sat back and smiled, her gaze bouncing to her American companion. "Thank goodness Mr. White agreed to help me, or I wouldn't be able to pull it off."

Sir Nathaniel chuckled some more. "Tell me…what is the surprise?"

She pulled her chin back in mock insult. "I won't say. Why, that would ruin everything."

"Of course. Of course." He dissolved into more laughter and leaned forward to slap Mr. White's knee several times. "Imagine that. A surprise."

"Imagine that." He gave Moira a slight jab. Looking her way, he rolled his eyes, causing her to giggle softly.

Thank God Sir Nathanial is in good humor tonight. One catastrophe averted. Hopefully no more would follow.

After some twenty minutes of polite chitchat, they reached Sir Nathaniel's quarters. Mr. White promised to see Moira back home and pay the driver for the hack. The older man was pleased with the plan and whistled all the way to his front entrance.

Mr. White swung himself across the way and took the vacated place opposite her. He leaned back against the bench and churned out a long sigh. "The man is particularly affable after a few glasses of rum and good food in his belly."

"And did I pass my *first test*?"

"Yes, and I congratulate you on your quick thinking."

"That's the nicest thing anyone's ever told me." Moira hid her wide smile by focusing on the passing scene outside the window. Lamplights glowed at front entrances and people strolled along the streets, mostly men.

"Surely you have heard better compliments than that."

"Nay, I have not. My parents didn't believe in what they called *puffing me up with vain words*, but I always knew when they approved or disapproved, by their expressions."

"I find that quite sad."

"What, that flattery leads to vanity and pride?" Moira shrugged. "It's true, and it's been many a good woman's downfall."

"Name one."

"Queen Marie Antoinette."

"Hmm..."

"She lived a life where those closest to her fueled her pride to the point where she couldn't see her people's needs, couldn't hear their cries as they starved in the streets."

"Well, I cannot disagree with you." As the carriage passed

a well-lit row of establishments, Moira glimpsed the smile on Mr. White's face. "You, Miss Kingsley, are quick-witted and intelligent. You will go far."

"Thank you." A blush set fire to her cheeks.

"So now I shall begin your official training." Mr. White leaned forward. "As a spy."

Moira's lips ached to smile with the pleasure threatening to burst from inside of her, but she controlled her emotion. Being a spy, after all, was serious business.

They rolled on in silence for quite some time. All was dark outside the carriage window; the only light emanated from the carriage's two outer lamps, which threw long eerie shadows at them. The air turned heavy, filled with the fresh, salty scent of the sea. It evoked a myriad of memories, but Moira forced them into the smallest corner of her mind. Were they about to board a ship bound for the American colonies?

Despite all the questions swirling in her brain, Moira said not a word. And she wouldn't cave to her growing sense of trepidation. However, she sensed that Mr. White wouldn't toss her into the sea as he threatened, and she would be free from marrying a man whose very presence made her skin crawl. The outcome was well worth the risk.

A short while later, the coach jerked to a halt.

"Wait here." Mr. White opened the carriage door and disappeared into the night.

Moira fought to control her excitement. She tried to recall all she'd heard about the New World and the colonists. Many were still dedicated to the Crown. She'd have to take special care to avoid them, lest they turn her over to Uncle Tyrus again.

The carriage door opened suddenly, giving Moira a start. Mr. White leaned inside and offered his hand. She placed her gloved fingers in his palm and climbed from the carriage.

"Miss Kingsley, allow me to present Mr. John Huff."

She regarded the slim man and replied with a small but polite curtsy.

"He's a trustworthy dockhand who will see to it that your valise finds its way aboard the *Seahawk*."

"I thank you, sir."

He gave a snort and eyed Mr. White. "You're sure 'bout this, Sam?"

An impatient-sounding sigh parted Mr. White's lips. "Quite sure. Now do the job I paid you to do."

"Aye." The barrel-chested Mr. Huff grumbled but did Mr. White's bidding.

Mr. White tossed a couple of coins to the carriage driver, who then slapped the reins and the vehicle pulled away.

"Now, Miss Kingsley, your first official lesson is about to begin, so pay attention."

"I shall hang on to your every word."

He offered his arm and Moira slipped her hand around his elbow, allowing him to guide her into an establishment called The Hungry Bear. One step inside and a glimpse of the surroundings told Moira that Papa would disapprove of the place. Beneath a smoky haze, women with ratted hair and immodest dresses milled about. Men bellied up to the bar and drank from large glasses of ale or rum. The latter's pungent order mingled with the smell of baked biscuits and hung heavily in the air. Mr. White removed his hat and led her to a table. He politely held out a banged-up wooden chair.

Moira sat, noting that, besides the working women, she was the only female in the place. It was on the tip of her tongue to ask if Mr. White intended to leave her there, but she remembered he'd said only minutes ago that her valise would be loaded onto a ship.

One of the serving wenches sashayed to the table and rubbed Mr. White's shoulders before leaning against him seductively. "What's your pleasure tonight, mister?"

He untangled her arms and moved her away. "Two plates of the house special. One glass of elderberry wine for the lady, and I'll have a cup of ale."

The working woman noticed Moira, seemingly for the first time. Moira took no offense. She was accustomed to surprised reactions. Papa used to joke that Moira was an invisible fairy that only special people of God could see.

No doubt she'd make a perfect spy.

The serving wench sauntered off, presumably to fetch their supper.

Mr. White leaned forward. "Have you taken note of the women in this place?"

"Of course." Moira jerked her chin at such an insult. "I have two eyes."

"Don't judge them too harshly. Life is difficult for women without means to live. Many of these soiled doves are mothers during the day and harlots at night while their children sleep, unaware of their mothers' professions."

"I do not judge them or anyone else. That is the Almighty's job, not mine."

"And how much money do *you* have, Miss Kingsley? How do you plan to pay for your passage and even your supper tonight?"

"I have plenty of money." Did she? "It's not on my person, but…"

"But what?" Mr. White sat back and folded his arms.

"My father left me an inheritance."

"And where is it?"

31

"I assume it's in the bank."

"Hmm…" Frown lines creased Mr. White's forehead. "That does pose a problem, doesn't it?"

Moira shifted, feeling uncomfortable now. She'd never had to consider her finances before. "Yes, I suppose it does."

The serving wench carried a large tray to their table and deposited two plates of food and the drinks in front of them. The smell rising from what appeared to be beef stew was not at all unpleasant and Moira's stomach rumbled, reminding her she'd had very little to eat today.

Mr. White caught the woman's wrist as she turned to go. "Tell us your name that we may leave a word of recommendation for you with your employer."

Her smile looked rather mechanical. "Dolly is m'name, sir."

"And, Dolly, do tell how you came to be working here?"

She yanked her hand free. "None of yer business how and why. Do you think I'd be here if I had a choice?"

Mr. White gave a careless shrug and Dolly scurried away.

His gaze slid to Moira and she realized she'd learned her first lesson. She had no money to pay for her escape aboard the *Seahawk*, no coin to cover her meal. In short, she was in no better situation than Dolly.

"I find myself in quite the conundrum, Mr. White."

"I'm glad you realize it."

Moira arched a brow. "But you have known it all along, haven't you?"

He nodded and lifted his fork. "We best eat whilst the food is hot."

Moira closed her eyes and murmured a quick prayer of thanks and then ate the surprisingly tasty stew atop a biscuit. After devouring half her portion, she couldn't eat another bite.

Mr. White waved Dolly over.

"Now what?" she said, her hands on her broad hips.

"Do you know a man…the Baron Kingsley?"

Dolly snickered. "Of course. All us girls know him."

Moira's face suddenly felt like she'd been in the sun too long. Surely the woman wasn't referring to Uncle Tyrus. He was a pillar of righteousness.

Wasn't he?

"The baron graces us with his presence at least once a week."

Moira's heart skipped. *Surely not!*

"Isn't it true that Baron Kingsley had come down in the world until his niece came to live with him?"

"'Tis true, all right. He owed everyone money. But the hearsay is his niece brought with her an inheritance in the nick of time." Dolly tossed her head and the straw-like mass on top of it barely moved. "And the baron is doin' his best to spend it, that he is. Why, he's been right generous to me."

Moira's mouth fell open. How dare this woman spout such lies! She glanced at Mr. White, whose darkened gaze warned her to keep quiet.

"And what of this prince of a fellow…a Major Nettles? I met him this evening. He's to marry the wealthy niece."

"Prince, indeed!" Dolly snickered. "I've got a six-inch scar on me breast that says he ain't no prince." She glanced Moira's way. "He likes to swordplay, you see, and he got a bit too…*playful*. I thought he'd cut me in two."

"The knave!" Moira had no problem believing Dolly's story. "What a horrid, evil man."

"Pity the niece." The serving wench shamelessly pulled down her already low-set neckline. "Look what he done to me. Just look!"

"I see." Moira swallowed hard, her gaze fixed on the fat pink scar running downward on the harlot's well-rounded, pale flesh.

"Imagine what the man will do to a wife? She'll be his property, to do with as he wishes."

"Yes, I can imagine." She sank back in her chair, praying her escape plans would somehow come to fruition.

But that raised the issue of money again.

Mr. White pressed a coin into Dolly's waiting palm. "Thank you for your time."

She inspected the coin. "Anytime." She adjusted her bodice and sent Mr. White a seductive look. To his credit, Mr. White didn't return the gesture.

Moira lowered her gaze and studied the scarred tabletop.

"So what have you to say of all this, Miss Kingsley?"

Moira brought her gaze to his. "I have learned that I'm penniless as we speak, while my uncle is scandalously spending my inheritance." She bit down hard, trying to contain her anger. *Be angry and sin not* as God's Word said. But Papa would be outraged if he knew what Uncle Tyrus did with the money he'd set aside for her.

She reclaimed her emotions. "I'm also certain now that my suspicions of Major Nettles are no longer suspicions, and I wish for escape more than ever." She tipped her head. "But how?"

Mr. White drained his mug. "Never fear, Miss Kingsley. We only have one visit to make tonight and all will be well." He leaned toward her and rewarded her with a charming smile. "I have thought of everything."

Chapter Four

••••ᡣᢙ♥ᡣᢙ••••

"How much farther?"

"Almost there, Miss Kingsley."

The second hired coach of the evening bumped along macadamized roads as they reached the city of London and now rode through the streets. Then quite suddenly, the driver pulled his team to a halt. Mr. White climbed out of the carriage and assisted Miss Kingsley's descent before handing the driver a coin. "Wait here. We shan't be too long."

The driver tugged on his low-slung cap.

Sam offered his arm and Miss Kingsley took it.

"Of all the nerve! Spending my inheritance on loose living. My uncle should be ashamed!"

"I should say so." She was angry. Good. A smirk tugged at the corners of his lips and he gave in to it.

Miss Kingsley fairly stomped her way up the walkway of her uncle's banker's home. Sam had it on good report that the man, Mr. George Golsby, kept an enormous amount of coin in his home office's vault, should Baron Kingsley or other clients get themselves into trouble after hours or should one of those aristocrats be forced to pay off an unfortunate who would not be a welcomed sight in the local branch of the Bank of England. Though Miss Kingsley was hardly an unfortunate, she couldn't exactly march into the bank and demand her funds.

But she could pay Mr. Golsby a surprise visit this evening and catch him off guard.

They reached the front entrance, marked by a red door. Sam unbuttoned his tailcoat, making sure his pistol was secure and at a moment's reach.

Miss Kingsley noticed the weapon. "You don't really plan to shoot him, do you?"

"I don't plan to, no." Sam gave the brass doorknocker a few good raps. He inhaled deeply. This had to go well.

Miss Kingsley lifted her chin and pushed back her slender shoulders.

A middle-aged maid answered the door.

"We're here to see Mr. Golsby, please," Sam said. "It's important."

"At this hour?" The maid brought her chin back so quickly it threatened the mobcap topping her head of brown curls. "The Golsbys are readying themselves for dinner."

"It won't take long. Tell him that Baron Kingsley's niece is here to see him."

The woman slammed the door in their faces.

Sam hurled a glance upward.

"How dare she shut us out like stray cats that mewed on the threshold!" Miss Kingsley gave a toss of her head. "Why, had she any manners, she'd have invited us into the parlor."

"I agree. No manners at all." Sam hoped to fuel her righteous indignation.

Minutes later, the door reopened and the maid, looking somewhat shamefaced, beckoned them inside.

Mr. Golsby met them in the long, narrow foyer. "Well, well, to what do I owe this surprise?" He looked from Sam to Miss Kingsley.

"I'm here to collect my inheritance, if you please."

Sam coughed. That's not the way he meant this conversation to begin. "What she means is…"

"Allow me." She took a step toward Mr. Golsby. "I'm Baron Kingsley's niece, Miss Moira Kingsley. My father was a missionary in Uganda. I'm sure you heard that he and my mother were killed in a fiery uprising, brought on by a rival tribe."

"A tragedy to be sure." Impatience hung on the man's every syllable. "But what has that to do with your inheritance or me?" He tipped his head. "And aren't you supposed to be at your engagement party? My family and I would have come, but my wife's parents are visiting from France."

"Then we'd best get this matter over with." Miss Kingsley stepped nearer to Golsby, her willowy frame nearly towering over him. "My father did not intend for my uncle to squander that money on imbibing and womanizing—and at The Hungry Bear, no less!"

Golsby sputtered.

Sam folded his arms. So far so good.

"I have evidence of this habit, sir, and if you refuse to give me my inheritance, I shall go to the newspaper."

Newspaper? Sam lifted his chin, thought it over, and let the threat dangle.

"Now, see here, Miss Kingsley!" Golsby's face turned crimson by degrees beneath the ensconced lighting. "This is my home, and—"

"I shall leave it at once and never return if you'll kindly give me my inheritance—or what's left of it."

"Where is your uncle? He is your guardian—and Major Nettles is your intended."

"Not anymore. My father would have never allowed me to marry such a man. One who cuts up women with the tip of his sword."

"Where did you hear such an outlandish tale?"

"'Tis no tale, sir, but a fact. I saw the scar with my own eyes."

Miss Kingsley's shoulders rose as she sucked in a deep breath. Sam thought she meant to shout and he moved to take her elbow. Losing her patience would accomplish nothing.

"Give me my inheritance or I shall go to the newspaper this very night!" She whispered the words but in such a way as to raise even Sam's hackles.

He almost pitied Golsby.

"And I shall name names," she added.

"George?" Another feminine voice floated up from behind Golsby. "George, what's this about?" A woman in a pearl silk gown appeared.

"Nothing, my dear. Go on back to the parlor. I shall join you shortly."

"Would our guests like to stay for dinner?" The woman's gaze fastened on Sam in a way that said she wouldn't mind some flirtation.

Sam looked away and pretended to study the nearby framed oil on canvas while keeping aware of Golsby's movement. He sensed the man might produce a pistol at any moment. After all, the contentious subject would impact him financially.

Golsby introduced his wife.

"I'm Baron Kingsley's niece, ma'am, and this is my...my *husband,* Samuel Wainwright."

What? Sam hid his shock by bowing politely.

"How is he your husband?" Golsby boomed. "You're betrothed to Major Nettles!"

Miss Kingsley clutched Sam's arm. "Well, you see, no one ever asked me about the engagement to Major Nettles. If they had, I would have confessed to my clandestine courtship with Samuel here." She batted her eyes at him and Sam battled the urge to grin.

All the while the Golsbys stared at Miss Kingsley as if she'd spoken a foreign language.

"We were married recently, you see"—her voice sounded smooth and sweet, like honey—"and we planned to confess the truth to everyone at the party tonight, but then I found out what Uncle Tyrus has been doing with my inheritance. Gaming and whoring!" The edge returned to her tone.

Mrs. Golsby gasped and clutched her throat.

"What's more, I seem to recall my father stating that I would gain access to my funds once I married or turned twenty-one. As you're aware, I'm only eighteen. However, I am married."

Ahh...

Sam understood the reason for her fib at once and decided to play along. He put his arm around her shoulders and pulled her close to him. "Be calm, my darling. If Mr. Golsby refuses to cooperate, we can always take the matter to the courts—after we go to the newspaper tonight."

Miss Kingsley stared up at him with a sudden vulnerability shining in her eyes. It felt quite natural to place a kiss on her forehead.

"Go to the newspaper?" Mrs. Golsby shrieked. "What would you say to them?"

"I would say..." Her gray eyes turned stone-like before she

gazed at the Golsbys. "Baron Tyrus Kingsley is a fraud. He is not an upstanding man. Nor is Major Nettles, who scarred a servicing wench with some sort of illicit swordplay. Baron Kingsley is not wealthy either, but has been scandalously spending his deceased missionary brother's funds, which were donated by God-fearing people who intended for the money to further God's kingdom." She took a breath. "That's what I'd say. For starters. Then I'd name the people involved with such spending. I would say—"

"My darling, I think the Golsbys understand your intentions." Enough chitchat. They had a ship to board. Sam pointed a stare at Mr. Golsby. "And now my wife will collect her inheritance—or what's left of it."

Golsby said nothing, but pulled a ring of keys on a chain from his tailcoat's front pocket. He headed down the adjoining hall.

"Wait here," Sam whispered to his *wife-in-lie*. Then he followed Golsby to be sure *his beloved* got every coin she owned.

"I'm coming too." She trailed Sam so closely that she bumped into him when he halted.

He turned. "Stay here and make sure Mrs. Golsby doesn't send for the authorities. Distract her. Tell her of your father and his work."

She nodded.

Good girl. Sam allowed himself a smirk. Miss Kingsley might make a good spy after all.

••••⟨❦⟩••••

It seemed like days since Mr. White had left her in the company of Mrs. Golsby and her French parents. Moira feared he'd escaped out the back door with her funds. Had this been a colossal prank, of which she'd been the target?

Her stomach churned, threatening to spill its contents onto the Golsbys' expensive oriental carpet, when she imagined herself trying to explain to Uncle Tyrus and tell him how she'd trusted a man she knew nothing about. He'd call her a little fool—and he would be correct!

Except escape had tasted so sweet...

"My dear, you look unwell."

Moira yanked herself from her musings and looked at Mrs. Golsby.

"Are you feeling poorly?"

She managed a smile. "Nay, I-I feel fine. Thank you."

To her parents, both quite elderly, Mrs. Golsby spoke in French. "She is a pathetic little sparrow, *n'est-ce pas?* But her husband is so handsome. She cannot expect him to remain faithful."

Moira understood every word and, as she'd been trained from a child on, answered the insult with Scripture. "Car c'est l'amour de Dieu, que nous gardions ses commandements." *For this is the love of God, that we keep his commandments.* To Mrs. Golsby, she added, "God said, 'Husbands, love your wives, even as Christ also loved the church, and gave himself for it.' So you see, I don't expect to keep him faithful. My trust is in the Lord, who shall do that particular work for me."

After the surprise of her use of the French language wore off, Mrs. Golsby gave a derisive-sounding snort.

But the old Frenchman grinned. "A wise girl," he muttered in his native tongue.

The reply caused deep creases on Mrs. Golsby's forehead. "I do hope our dinner is not getting cold."

Moira shifted. Another wave of nervous flutters caused her heart to trip over itself. If Sam didn't return soon, her Bible recitation would ring hollow and all of England would label her a hypocrite. What's more, they'd be poor. Uncle Tyrus would banish her to the workhouse in London, a dismal place, she'd heard. And worst of all, her father's good name would be ruined.

Why, oh why, had she not considered this sooner?

She lowered her head and squeezed her eyes closed. *Oh, Lord, forgive—*

"Come, darling, it's time to go."

Hearing the smooth, low timbre of a man's voice, Moira snapped to attention. She glanced up at Sam and dizzying relief filled her being.

"Our business here is finished."

Moira took his proffered hand and stood. The room tilted at an odd angle. Sam's eyes widened, his arm locked around her waist, and he whisked her outside.

"Breathe deeply, Miss Kingsley," he whispered close to her ear. "All went well."

Chapter Five

"Are you feeling all right?"

Safely within the confines of the carriage and now on their way to the wharf, Moira never felt better. "I'm fine, Mr. White. Thank you. I experienced a moment's panic is all."

"Ah…" Mr. White leaned toward her so his shoulder pressed against hers. "Well I must admit, Mr. Golsby certainly took his sweet time delivering up your inheritance." Reaching into his tailcoat, he produced a black velvet pouch and placed it into her gloved palm. "Allow me to present what's left of your inheritance. I'm sure Golsby held out on us, although the funds he parted with ought to last long enough for you to find employment in the United States."

"Employment?"

"Yes." He nudged her playfully. "We spies do not earn a living, I'm afraid. We must hold regular positions like everyone else."

"Wh-what can I do?" She'd never had to consider obtaining employment.

"A teacher? A governess? Do either of those appeal to you?"

"Oh, yes." Moira perked up. "I have experience with both."

"Perfect."

Moira smiled. The bag of coins weighed heavily in her hand. She had no pockets in the gown she wore and only a shawl graced her shoulders. "Will you keep this safe for me, Mr. White?"

"Of course." He tucked the velvet pouch in what surely was an inside pocket of his tailcoat. "You will need to sew pockets into your undergarments so you can safely carry your coins on your person."

"I packed a reticule."

"Reticules can easily be stolen. However, even if miscreants steal the gown off your back, your money will be safely hidden in your undergarments."

Moira gasped.

"Forgive my bluntness."

She narrowed her gaze. "Lesson two in my spy schooling, I imagine."

Mr. White chuckled, a deep rumbling sound that was not at all unpleasant. "Lesson two indeed."

The stench of rotting fish and human waste permeated the air and indicated they neared the wharf. She vaguely recalled it from her passage to England after her parents were killed. When she'd finally come to herself in Uncle Tyrus's home, she was told she'd been in shock for weeks, which explained why she only recalled bits and pieces of the voyage.

But this smell of the wharf…it brought back her intense dread of the wide, rolling, deep sea. The fear coiled around her insides like a deadly serpent. Papa called her feelings of panic "unfounded," and Moira supposed that described it well enough.

The carriage pulled to a halt and Mr. White climbed out. Moira took his proffered hand and alighted. He then paid the driver and the conveyance pulled away.

Mr. White directed her attention to a ship bobbing out on the dark water. From this vantage point, it looked like a harmless child's toy. "There she is. The *Seahawk*."

"Has it left without us?"

"No. She's merely moored a ways out, as she's all loaded and ready to sail come morning. We must pray for a good gust of wind." He glanced up and down the wharf. "In the meantime, we'll have to find a rowboat to get us out there."

Moira's stomach flipped. She detested rowboats. However, staying in England was not an option.

Lord, help me. She'd had nightmares of drowning in the sea.

"Miss Kingsley?"

She shook herself. "Yes?"

"Over here." Mr. White led her to a scruffy-looking sailor who greeted him like he was an old friend.

"Happy to oblige you, Sam. We'll get you out to the *Seahawk* straightaway. Climb aboard." The slender man's gaze openly appraised Moira, bringing heat to her cheeks. "She comin' too?"

"She is."

"That'll be double the price."

Sam retrieved several coins from a pocket in his waistcoat, counted them, then placed them in the man's outstretched palm. Even in the glimmering moonlight, she could tell the man was unkempt—and he smelled as bad as the wharf itself.

Sam stepped into the rowboat and reached for Moira. Lifting her gown slightly, she climbed aboard the jouncing vessel. She clung to Sam's arm and he planted her on a plank bench. The sailor hopped in and shoved off.

"You must no longer call me *Mr. White*." He spoke softly near Moira's right ear, sending tingles down her spine. "It's my pseudonym, and I don't wish to have it known on the ship."

"I see." Moira frowned. "What shall I call you?"

"Stryker. Mr. Sam Stryker."

"Another pseudonym?" Her frown deepened.

"No, my real name." As if sensing her confusion, her captor added, "The captain of the *Seahawk* knows me, knows of my…eh, *business,* and even supports my endeavors when possible." He pointed toward the ship. "But see how she flies the Union Jack?"

Moira nodded. "British vessels do."

"That flag will be hauled down as soon as we're on the high seas and the Stars and Stripes will wave in its place."

Moira leaned close. "A spy ship?"

"More or less." A smile lightened his tone.

"Should I have a pretend identity, Mr. White—I mean…Mr. Stryker?"

He paused, and she stared into his night-darkened features. "I would be honored if you would call me Sam," he said just above a whisper. "We will be shipmates for at least six weeks."

"That long?"

"That long."

Moira swallowed as the rowboat crested a wave and pitched forward. Mr. White—Sam—took hold of her waist and steadied her as water sloshed over the sides. A salty spray moistened her face, but she felt safe as Sam held her close to him.

The sailor behind them grunted as he rowed, nearing them

to the ship.

"If I'm to call you by your given name, then you must call Moira." She had to lean back in order to catch Sam's expression.

"As you wish...*Moira*."

He spoke her name almost intimately, and shivers of delight washed over her as powerful as any wave. She felt mesmerized, until she reminded herself that this man was an American spy, more of a stranger than a confidant.

Except she felt like she'd known him her entire life.

The *Seahawk* suddenly loomed high above them as they reached its mooring. The sailor called to other men on board and they looked over the side.

"I've got two more here, requestin' to come aboard. I believe you'll be knowing ol' Sam, here, and he's got a woman with him."

A bit of banter ensued above them, followed by activity, and then a rope ladder fell over the side of the ship.

"There ya be, Sam."

"Appreciate it. And take this..." Wearing a grin, Sam turned and chucked a coin to the boatman. "I'd also be grateful if you forget you saw me and the lady here tonight."

"Forgotten." The older man's raspy chuckle rivaled the wind, the splashing water, and the men's voices high above them. "Me memory ain't so good these days an'how."

Sam stood and made his way to the edge of the rowboat. He grabbed hold of the ladder with one hand and reached for Moira with the other. "You'll need to remove your gloves lest you slip."

She pulled off one, then the other while gauging the challenge before her. It was a straight-up climb, while most ladders were at an angle to ease the effort. "You don't expect me to go up that thing, do you?"

"I do, yes." Sam took her gloves and tucked them into his coat. "And you will."

Moira stared at his outstretched hand. "But—"

Before she could utter another syllable he grabbed her hand and yanked her toward the unstable ladder.

"My hems will not allow me a wide gait," she whispered, although it came out as something of a hiss.

"Pull them to your knees then."

"I beg your pardon!" She glanced at the sailor in the rowboat, who chuckled at her dilemma. "I will not have him"—she nodded toward the stern of the rowboat—"looking at my legs while I make a very undignified, if not impossible, climb."

"I will block the view," Sam promised. "I will be right behind you."

"You will not!" She tried to keep her voice lowered despite the exclamation.

"Well, I can't go first. How will I catch you if you should slip and fall into the water?"

A paralyzing fear crept down her spine.

Sam reached for the ladder and pulled the rowboat right up to the tall ship.

"I ain't got all night here!"

Sam looked at their rowboat captain. "Give us a few more moments, if you please." He bent his head close to Moira. "He is losing his patience and soon the crew of the *Seahawk* will too." After placing her slippered foot onto one of the wooden rungs, he forced her palms around the rough edges of another one. "Up you go, Moira."

Her knees weakened and suddenly she felt cool air on her legs. She felt Sam close behind her.

"Freedom is merely a few rungs away." Sam's voice penetrated the fog of fear. "You can do this, and I'll be right behind you."

"C'mon, missy," a sailor shouted somewhere above her. "We'll haul you over if you can climb high enough for us to reach you."

Determination overstepped her anxiety and Moira shot her left hand up to the next rung. Taking great care, she lifted her left leg. Then her right.

"That's a girl. You can do it." It seemed the whole crew cheered her upward.

Except the ladder seemed to stretch on for miles.

Freedom is merely a few rungs away. Sam's words propelled her onward. After all, getting rowed back to shore and returning to her life with Uncle Tyrus, Aunt Aggie, and Major Nettles was an impossibility now that she'd tasted liberty.

And given the choice of that or drowning, she'd prefer the latter.

She climbed higher, the muscles in her arms quivering from the unaccustomed overuse. She managed two more rungs before her strength vanished. She couldn't climb another inch. But a hand on her bottom thrust her upward and many pairs of hands clamped onto her arms. Through no effort of her own, she was lifted over the side of the *Seahawk*.

"Light as a feather, ye are." a sailor said. "Take care ye don't blow away on a gust o' wind."

Her feet landed on the deck and she teetered like a drunken man before finding a nearby railing. She quickly pulled her petticoat and gown to their rightful places at her ankles.

Within seconds, it seemed, Sam was aboard. Relief showered over her. They'd made it!

A dark-haired man stepped forward and, by the look of his coat and accoutrements, Moira guessed he was the captain.

He and Sam shook hands and then Sam indicated Moira.

"I've only one cabin left," the captain said before introductions could even be made. He sent Moira what seemed a rueful look. Back to Sam, he added, "I'm loaded deep and took on other passengers. There's no room for one more person. I wish you'd have contacted me before bringing your lady friend aboard."

"No need for an extra room, Captain." Sam's gaze locked on Moira. He cleared his throat. "This is my wife…Mrs. Samuel Stryker."

While the captain and crew clapped Sam on the back and called their congratulations, dread poured over Moira. It was one thing to fib about marriage in order to obtain her inheritance but quite another to share a cabin with a man outside of wedlock.

Sam made his way over to her and wrapped his arm around her shoulders. "Come, darling. I'll show you to our cabin."

Chapter Six

••••👂••••

Lamp in hand, Sam led Miss Kingsley—Moira—below deck. He was usually fortunate enough to acquire a cabin, although he wasn't above sleeping in the steerage with the crew. But that was no place for a lady.

Sam reached for Moira's hand as they made their way quietly through the deserted passageway. Entering their tiny cabin, he saw her lips move as if she wanted to protest, but he closed the cabin door before nary a word could be uttered and hung the lamp on a long spike in the wall. He then took in their cramped quarters. Nothing had changed since he'd sailed nearly a year ago.

"Welcome to our home for the next six weeks or so." He glimpsed her horrified expression and grinned. In truth, Sam couldn't imagine how this would work, but they'd have to attempt it—and succeed.

"I…I…" Evidently she'd been rendered speechless.

"You may sleep in the bunk," Sam whispered, recalling the thin plank walls dividing the cabins. "I'll make a pallet on the floor."

"Six weeks…together?"

"Could be more like eight without a tailwind."

"Oh, my, this will never do!"

"Shh…you must keep your voice low, lest crewmen overhear."

"That's two months." She whispered the words this time.

Sam chuckled at her inability to keep up with the conversation. "We'll make the best of it, hmm?" He tipped his head. "Unless you'd prefer to return to the mainland before we set sail. I'm sure I could commission one of the crew to take you back."

"No!" She lifted her chin with obvious determination and ran her palms down the skirt of her gown as if doing so manufactured more dignity than their situation dictated. "I will adapt."

"I've no doubt." He didn't either—which was why he'd so easily lied to Harney and his crew.

"This will serve as lesson three in my spy schooling, no doubt."

Sam grinned.

She cocked her head, studying him. "Your last name is Stryker. Like the explorer?"

"A relation, I'm told." Sam smiled at her confused expression.

"So how did you come to possess the. surname White? A flip of a coin, perhaps?"

"No, actually, my father was English." Sam supposed she didn't need to hear of his heritage, but thought it worthy enough to share nonetheless. "My mother is Catawba Indian. Her people call me 'Whitefeather' because of a streak of white in my otherwise brown hair."

"Ah, so you shortened it to White."

Sam nodded, placed his hands on his hips, and glanced

around. His sea chest and Moira's valise had arrived and now sat in the corner of the tiny cabin.

"Please…" Moira stepped forward. "If we are to spend so much time together, will you tell me something of yourself?"

"I just did."

Moira leaned against the makeshift desk. "Do you have siblings?"

"One brother, Asher, who returned to the Catawba people along with my mother."

Moira's brow puckered. "What about your father?"

"Dead." Sam tasted bitterness on his tongue and a renewed sense of purpose. "My father, a good man, was a blacksmith in a remote village outside of Charleston, South Carolina. One afternoon in broad daylight, two men, both British, shot him dead after he refused to shoe their horses on the spot." Sam pulled in a long breath. "My father sensed the men were up to no good. He was right." Sam clenched his fist, remembering. "As it happened, the two were spying for the Crown. They spent a few nights in jail for killing my father, but were released by a judge partial to King George." With a wag of his head, he added, "They walked free."

"And now you avenge your father's death by turning the tables on the British?"

"That, and more." Sam saw compassion in her gaze. "I have my mission." And, God willing, he'd get to Washington City before the British did.

"I see." She stepped toward him, wringing her hands. "Then with British sympathizers in high positions, I will be in danger of being turned over to my uncle."

"That won't happen."

"How can you know?" She stared off somewhere beyond him. "I fear Uncle Tyrus will do anything to get my inheritance under his control again. Perhaps he'll say I've lost my senses because I ran off with you." Her shoulders sagged and her gaze returned to Sam. "So I'll not find refuge on American soil after all? "

"You shall find refuge."

A frown settled on her features. "But, the British..."

"Not all American cities side with the Crown. Quite the opposite. Many of the First Nations, like the Catawba people, side with the Americans also."

A shadow fell across her features. "My parents and I loved the tribal people of Uganda. I'm sure I will feel quite at home with your people."

Sam lifted a halting hand. He didn't plan to take Moira with him. After they docked, she was on her own. "After this voyage, you'll find yourself in either Washington City or Alexandria, and you'll surely find some position that suits you."

"Oh...of course." Disappointment shone in her eyes. "Pardon my presumption."

Sam arched a brow. "You didn't think that I would deposit you with the Catawba, did you?"

"I'm afraid I don't know what to think at the moment."

"I've every confidence you'll figure out a purpose by the time we reach the United States." He smiled. "However, we must survive this voyage without giving ourselves away, so there is something we must agree on." He glanced at the doorway. They needed to take great care lest they be apprehended by sympathizers to the Crown when they docked. It would take no more than an eavesdropping crewman who would sell his own soul, not to mention Sam and Moira, for a coin. "We must make a vow to each other here and now." He stepped in so that he stood but half an arm's length away. He felt almost mesmerized by the way she looked up at him as flickering lamplight played across her features.

"What is this vow we must make?"

Sam blinked. "Never shall we be untruthful to each other. To others, yes, for the sake of our causes, but to one another, never."

"I dislike being untruthful at all."

Sam ran his forefinger along her jaw line, bringing it to rest beneath her chin. "So far, you have done a fine job *playacting*. Which reminds me…" He reached into his tailcoat, glad for the diversion. His thoughts wandered down a most dangerous path just now. Retrieving her money, he took her hand and placed the black velvet bag on her palm. "I believe this belongs to you."

She smiled up at Sam and his gaze caught the shiny curves of her mouth and lingered there. Perhaps just one kiss…

No, no, no! That would not do at all. He'd feel even more responsible for her then.

"Thank you."

Her whispered reply wound its way around Sam's heart. What the devil was wrong with him?

She tipped her head. "I can't help but wonder why you rescued me tonight and didn't kill me as you initially planned. I'm ever so grateful for it, of course, but I'm nothing. A no one of a female, engaged to a man she loathed the thought of marrying. Surely there are more like me, perhaps more worthy of your benevolence."

"Perhaps, but my benevolence found you." He bestowed on her what he hoped was a charming grin and topped it off with a gallant bow.

His reward was her smile—a smile that reached her eyes, like when they'd danced.

"But why, Mr. Samuel Stryker? Tell me."

He wasn't sure he could put his motives into words. "Let's just say I'm partial to damsels in distress and leave it there, shall we?"

"As you wish."

"Now with those particulars out of the way, I'll leave you to relax and unpack your valise." Sam nodded to where it sat atop his sea chest.

He moved toward the door, intending to find some rum and an over-talkative sailor willing to divulge secrets.

His best bet was Harney.

And, of course, he'd have to give a special hello to Rachel.

"One last question and I'll not raise the subject again."

With his hand on the doorknob, he cast a backwards glance, waiting.

"How many damsels have you rescued thus far?"

He smirked. "Only one, my fair daisy. Only one."

Chapter Seven

....⟨❤⟩....

After two days at sea, the nausea finally left Moira. What's more, she finally seemed to find her sea legs, although from time to time she still teetered like a drunken man. Tonight, however, the ship seemed to barely sway, and the promise of a gulp of fresh air lured her from her cramped quarters.

She made her way down the companionway, hearing men singing some jolly tune in the cabin next to hers. Reaching the stairs, she clung to the railing and climbed to the upper deck. As soon as her nose hit the night air, she breathed in deeply of its salty freshness. How stuffy the cabin had become!

Stuffy...and lonely.

Odd, life's latest turn of events. Before meeting Mr. Samuel Stryker, Moira had spent the majority of her time alone. While her parents were alive, they were her best friends as together they did God's work and ministered to various peoples. She didn't need others.

But then she met Sam on the night of her engagement party, and he loomed larger than life. Indeed, she had felt like a damsel in distress, and he was her knight in shining armor. But after they set sail, it seemed he had vanished. She'd only caught glimpses of him when he came and went in the mornings. Once he'd muttered something about a woman named Rachel. Could it be she occupied Sam's time?

'Twas none of her business whether she did or didn't.

Moira stepped out onto what she assumed was the main deck. Only a few lanterns lighted the starboard side. However, a full moon lit up even the darkest corners. Making her way to the side of the ship, she tested the railing and deemed it secure. Then she stared at God's handiwork. The moon loomed large, and Moira felt that if she reached out she could touch it where God had hung it in the sky. How gorgeous was its reflection upon the black, glassy sea. With her hands holding tightly to the railing, a smile twitched her lips. Were she an artist, such a vision would fill her canvas, and it would be a prized piece, indeed.

"You have ventured from the cabin, I see."

The voice gave Moira a start. Hands clamped firmly on her shoulders as if to keep her from falling overboard, although she maintained her death grip on the rough, wood railing. Recognition dawned.

"Mr. Stryker."

"Sam," he whispered close to her ear.

Moira inched away. Did he not have his time full with charming Rachel?

"I take it you're feeling better."

She nodded. A slight breeze stirred the loose strands of her hair. She'd long since given up hope of keeping it fastened with pins and had settled for one long braid that rested between her shoulder blades.

"Beautiful night, isn't it?"

"It is." She watched him, studying him, actually, as he leaned his forearms on the railing. If possible he'd grown more handsome since their voyage began. His hair was tied into a queue, although some shorter stands escaped the black band at his nape. He wore no tailcoat or overcoat and the arms of his white shirt billowed like sails as the light breeze caught the material.

"The calm sea is a nice reprieve after the rough ride of the last few days."

"Indeed."

He turned and regarded her with a crooked grin. "You weren't the only one retching."

"You too?"

He nodded.

"And how did Rachel fare?" Moira instantly regretted the challenging note in her tone. "I-I mean, it's nice to know there are other females onboard, but I hope she wasn't as sick as I."

"She's just fine. In her element, I'd say." Sam snorted a laugh. "I believe Rachel is as good a sailor as Harney."

"The captain?"

"Yes. And Rachel is anxious to meet you. She's been yearning for female companionship."

Moira forced a smile, although a sourness rose up and lodged in her chest. Why on earth would she want to meet such a woman as Rachel?

Worse, why did she feel jealous?

She shook off the notion. "Have you gotten any sleep since we left England?" she asked him.

"Here and there."

In Rachel's bunk? Moira pressed her lips together before such a question escaped. 'Twas no business of hers where the man slept.

"You bolted the cabin door." Sam's voice stole her attention. "I couldn't get in, and I knew you weren't feeling well, so I didn't want to wake you."

"I locked the door…" Guilt stabbed at her. "Oh, Sam, I'm truly sorry."

"Don't be." He turned and leaned his backside against the railing, crossed his booted ankles, then folded his arms. "I found an empty hammock in the steerage and met the passengers sailing with us."

"Oh?"

"All of them will be departing when we reach Portugal."

"Portugal?" Moira turned to face him. "But I thought we were headed to America."

"We are, but to throw off British officials, Harney logged his destination as Portugal. From there we will set a course due west for America."

"I see." Moira didn't much care where the captain chose to dock as long as her escape was complete. "I'm sorry for locking you out of your cabin, Sam."

"Again, no harm done." He flashed a charming smile. "As I said, I found an empty hammock."

Moira's envy vanished, and it seemed so petty an emotion. She forced a pleasant expression. "I look forward to meeting Rachel."

Sam inclined his head and splashes of moonlight danced off his golden brown hair. "You'll like her. She's as adventurous as you are."

"You see me as adventurous?"

"Oh, no, not a bit." Sam's voice dripped with sarcasm. "You ran away with a stranger to escape marrying a man you loathe, you claimed your inheritance, leaving your dishonest uncle without the means to which he's become accustomed this last half year, and you boarded a ship for a foreign land."

A giggle escaped her. "And I'm not a bit sorry either."

Sam chuckled. "Well, just in case you do have a tweak of conscience, I have every confidence that Mr. Golsby hoarded some funds for your uncle and himself."

"No doubt." Moira assumed so, and it did soothe her somewhat. She didn't want to harm her aunt and uncle, but had Uncle Tyrus not wasted her funds—and his own as well—he wouldn't find himself in a financial pinch.

"Thank you, Mr. Stryker. I'm grateful for all you've done for me."

"Sam," he growled.

"Thank you, Sam." She leaned close to him. "You're a fine coconspirator."

"Such compliments. You'll have me blushing."

Moira hurled a glance toward the starry sky. *Blushing, indeed!*

A long pause ensued and only the rhythmical sounds of water lapping against the ship reached Moira's ears. Above, metal chinked and clanked with each slight roll of the ship on the sea's calm current.

"There they are!" A deep male voice splintered the night. "The newlyweds."

Moira turned to see the captain heading their way. His back was devoid of its dark-blue tailcoat and, like Sam, he wore only his shirt tucked into dark breeches. Black boots covered his lower legs and feet.

"Glad you're feeling better, Mrs. Stryker." He came to a halt several feet away.

"I feel much better, thank you, sir."

"Good." He rubbed his palms together and looked from Moira to Sam. "Then I insist you both take breakfast with my wife and me in the morning." His gaze bounced back to Moira. Her empty stomach grumbled, reminding her she'd had little to eat the last forty-eight hours.

"What say you, my darling?" Sam stretched his arm across her shoulders.

Why did it feel so natural to lean into his embrace? Even the smell of him, all spice, and fresh air, seemed so familiar.

"I would like nothing more." After a smile at Sam, she inclined her head politely. "Thank you, Captain."

"My pleasure." He bent slightly at the waist. "Until tomorrow morning then."

"We'll be there," Sam promised.

Moira wondered when he would remove his arm. They were playacting, after all.

But he didn't. "Allow me to escort you back to our cabin."

"Thank you." She'd cleaned it as best she could after being sick for a couple of days, and a cabin boy named Anthony had been ever so caring, bringing her biscuits, water, and even hot tea. He had cleaned the chamber pot and mopped the floor, and Moira had never met a nicer boy.

They reached the cabin and Moira entered. She glanced behind her, but Sam hadn't followed.

"I'll be along later, so leave the door unlocked."

"I will…but where are you going?"

"I never turn in without visiting Rachel while I'm on board. I cannot pass up her, eh, midnight treats."

Moira whirled around and faced the wall so Sam wouldn't see the anger she felt. She clenched her jaw so hard her back teeth began to ache. The door closed, leaving her feeling oddly empty, jealous and angry—emotions she'd never dealt with before. No one before Sam had ever made her feel special in that certain way a lady longs to feel. Moira had seen it plenty of times, romance blooming between a man and young lady.

Oh, of course, she knew God loved her—but He had to.

He'd created her, after all. And Papa and Mum…they'd loved her too. In all her eighteen years, she'd been satisfied with that love—parental love. Heavenly love.

Why, then, did she suddenly want more?

···· ❧❦❧ ····

Sam opened the cabin door and crept inside. He set the lamp he carried down on the tiny writing desk and stared at the sight which greeted him. Moira lying on a pallet on the floor while the bunk sat empty, although its covers had been turned down.

He shook his head. It would never do.

He crept forward and hunkered down beside Moira. The steady rise and fall of her chest indicated that she slept. Gathering her in his arms, he stood and made his way to the bunk. She awakened as he set her onto the bed.

"What are you doing?"

"Moving you to the bunk where you belong."

"But you should have the bunk." Sleepiness caused her to slur a few words.

The topic, however, was not up for negotiation. "Goodnight, Moira." He got to his feet and began unbuttoning his shirt.

"Sam, please…"

He glanced over his shoulder.

"I've been praying, and I clearly saw how selfish I've been."

Sam frowned and placed his hands on his hips. "Selfish, how so?"

"I've been behaving as if this was my cabin, not yours. I locked you out and forced you to sleep in less favorable conditions."

"Moira, stop." He raised a hand, palm side out. "It was a

mistake on your part, that's all." He continued undressing. "I'd wager you don't have a selfish bone in your body."

"Oh, but I do. I even felt like…well…where you're concerned…"

"What about me?" Sam pulled off his muslin shirt, changing it for a clean one. When nothing more came from Moira, he faced her. "Well?"

"Never mind."

Sam sat on top of his sea chest and tugged off his boots. "For your information, and despite my five and twenty years, my mother would switch me if she learned I'd allowed a lady to sleep on the floor while I took a padded bunk."

The remark earned him a soft giggle. Sam grinned as images of his mother's stern face flashed in his mind. Suddenly he longed to see her again. He missed her and his brother Asher.

But for his duty, he'd return home.

He shook off the nostalgia and pulled off his socks.

"Good night, Sam Stryker."

"Good night, my darling daisy."

He pushed up off the sea chest and made his way to the pallet. He knelt and rearranged the blankets so that instead of running the width of the cabin, his bedding ran the length. He gathered the extra blanket and packed it beneath his head. A moan of relief escaped him. How good it felt to stretch out on a hard surface and without his boots.

He closed his eyes and fell asleep listening to Moira's soft, sweet snores.

Chapter Eight

Humming. He heard humming. He knew the tune, had sung the hymn. The words scampered through his mind.

Awake, my soul, and with the sun
Thy daily stage of duty run;
Shake off dull sloth, and joyful rise,
To pay thy morning sacrifice.

Sam opened one eye and saw Moira brushing her long, blond hair. It waved like strands of gold silk and hung to her narrow hips. Both eyes opened now, he watched, mesmerized, as she neatly divided her locks into three parts and began to braid each section. Her long, slender fingers worked expertly and, once she'd knotted each section, she took the three long pieces and braided them. The result was a fat braid which she knotted at her nape.

Standing from where she'd been sitting on his sea chest, she began to sing softly while retrieving a brown garment and several pieces of frippery from her valise. Her soprano had a soothing effect on Sam and he let his eyelids flutter close. He heard the rustling of clothing as Moira dressed and, though he longed to peek, he determined to give her a semblance of privacy.

But would he be able to keep his eyes closed for six weeks? The notion seemed impossible, especially since Sam had an affinity for the lady.

Well, more than an affinity. He would acknowledge that much. He was attracted to her, plain and simple. She'd sparked his curiosity from the start when he'd seen her standing in the shadows, wearing an expression of misery at her betrothal celebration. When he'd danced with her and made her smile, he'd felt a great measure of success. And later, when he'd resolved to take her with him, it seemed to solve both of their dilemmas. He didn't need to kill her and she wouldn't be forced to marry a devilish redcoat.

However, with those problems solved, a new one arose for Sam. One that affected his heart.

If only he could stop thinking about it—about her. Moira. He chanced a peek at her. She'd dressed in a drab brown gown. Seconds later, she donned a lacy ivory collar which cheered her ensemble somewhat. He admired her willowy, yet decidedly feminine, figure. He enjoyed her courage and wit. What a fool Nettles had been, although his loss could well be Sam's gain.

Except Sam was in no position to pursue a romance. He had a job to do. His president and countrymen were counting on him.

Now, would to God he'd get to Washington City before the British did.

Pounding at the door brought Sam fully awake. He grinned at Moira's startled expression.

He clambered to his feet. "Who is it?"

"It's Mr. Jamison."

"Ah, yes," he said softly to Moira. "The first mate."

"What does he want?" Moira whispered.

Sam shrugged and tossed his pallet of blankets onto the bunk, so as not to give away their marriage scheme. "What is it, Jamison?"

"I bring a message from the captain."

Wearing trousers and his un-tucked white shirt which hung to his knees, Sam collected his pistol and crossed the small cabin. He hid the weapon behind him and pulled open the door wide enough to reveal the bearded sailor on the other side.

"Breakfast will be ready in thirty minutes." He strained to see over Sam's shoulder without success as Sam stood taller than he did. "Your presence is requested."

Sam gave a nod. "We'll be there with time to spare."

•••• ᏅᏋ♥ᏋᎧ ••••

Moira followed Sam down the narrow companionway to the captain's quarters. They didn't have far to go.

"Why, it's on the other side of that little kitchen area we just passed."

"It's referred to as the galley, my darling daisy." Sam tossed her a grin before knocking at the captain's cabin door.

Young Anthony answered. "Come right in, if you please."

Moira smiled at the boy's formality.

"It's good to see you feeling better," the lad said. "You were looking awfully green for a while."

"I feel much better, thank you. You took good care of me."

Sam cupped her elbow and led her across the richly-paneled cabin. Two round windows appeared on the far wall and allowed in a flood of sunshine. They reached a beautiful ebony-haired woman with dancing brown eyes. "Moira, meet the best cook on the seven seas. Mrs. Rachel Harney."

"Such flattery, Sam." A pretty blush crept up the sides of

the woman's face.

Realization squeezed her gut and Moira swallowed hard. "You're Rachel, the captain's wife?"

"Yes, and, I believe you've met Anthony." Her tone was accented by what Moira guessed was Spanish. "He is our son."

"Oh…" An odd sense of relief washed over Moira. She covered her emotions by smiling at Anthony. "And a fine boy he is."

"Aye, and we're proud of him." Mrs. Harney's thick hair was folded into a braid and, similar to Moira's, it hung down her back. "I hope the two of us will become good friends. I already adore your husband, because it's so much fun to feed him." She gazed at Sam, but Moira saw no special or come-hither sparks.

"What can I say?" Sam lifted his shoulders. "I'm a growing boy and you're a marvelous cook."

Moira suddenly understood last night's pre-bedtime visit to Rachel.

The woman appeared quite pleased by the compliment. "Between you and Anthony I barely leave the galley." Her smile widened and her gaze fixed on Moira. "Do you cook, Mrs. Stryker?"

It took a heartbeat for her to realize Mrs. Harney addressed her. "Oh, yes, actually. I know my way around cooking fire and brick oven, although I fear the meals I prepare are merely adequate."

"Doesn't sound like you'll starve to death, Sam." Chuckling, Captain Harney crossed the large cabin and clapped Sam on the back. Next he politely greeted Moira and then introduced his first mate, Mr. Jamison, and a couple other crewmen. "Let's be seated, shall we?" He rubbed his palms together. "I despise a cold breakfast."

"Everything is ready, my husband." Rachel instructed a young dark-skinned man with straight black hair to commence serving the food. And then, when her expressive dark eyes met the captain's, something passed between them, something raw and undefined, and yet Moira had seen it before between lovers. How fortunate for Rachel that her husband openly adored her.

And, in that moment, Moira gained a healthy respect for the captain of the *Seahawk*. 'Twas a good man, indeed, who didn't hide his love for his wife. Papa cherished Mum, but he and Captain Harney were a rare breed. Most men, it seemed, equated such affection with weakness and considered marriage to be agreements of acquisition instead of the binding together of two hearts made whole.

Moira startled, feeling pressure on her elbow.

Sam stood beside her. "Shall we?" He indicated to the linen tablecloth with its many place settings.

"Thank you." She sent him a smile as he politely seated her.

He then took the chair to her right.

Anthony plopped himself into the chair on her left.

"A prayer of thanks, if you'll all bow your heads." Standing at the head of the table, the captain said grace.

And, oddly, for the first time since her parents perished, Moira felt like she...*belonged.*

Chapter Nine

····· ᎒Ꮬ♥ᏣᎧ ····

Near the railing at the side of the ship, Moira watched the goings-on beside Rachel. After ten long days, the *Seahawk* anchored off the Porto de Lisboa at last. The passengers who'd sailed as far as Portugal were ferried ashore by crewmen. Sam had decided he'd go ashore too, with hopes of finding a newspaper or hearing updates on the war between England and the Colonies.

"A beautiful day," Rachel remarked, lifting her face to the sunshine.

"Indeed." Moira saw Sam wave and replied in kind just before a hefty breeze blew strands of hair onto her face and across her eyes. She brushed them back with her fingers.

"I don't think I have ever seen two people more in love." Rachel's voice was as smooth as butter.

"Which two people?" Moira turned to her new friend.

"Why, you and Sam, of course."

The words took root and jumbled Moira's thoughts. "Sam and I?" In the last two weeks, she'd wished it were true, that she really was Sam Stryker's wife. He'd been a complete gentleman and treated her with respect. Moira felt she knew him better than almost anyone alive, and she'd grown quite fond of him. "Do you really think so?"

"Yes, of course." Rachel laughed as if Moira's response tickled her to the core. "Who else would I be speaking of? There's no other couple on board except Bob and me, and I don't know how we appear to others."

Moira smiled. "You and Captain Harney look very happy together."

"Likewise.." Rachel gave her a playful jab and laughed again.

Despite her smiles, Moira felt a tweak of conscience. Rachel, too, had become dear to her, and Moira hated the deceit.

"Come, let's move your belongings out of the first mate's cabin and into a larger, more comfortable one. Mr. Jamison will want his room back, now that the other passengers have debarked."

Moira followed Rachel below deck. She'd hoped Sam would have confessed his lies to the captain by now and explained their situation so they could sleep in separate cabins. However, Sam said it was too late for confessions; they'd have to live with the lie until they reached America. As for disembarking here at Port Lisbon, Sam advised against it. It wasn't far enough away from England, and Uncle Tyrus and Nettles would find her for sure. She'd pay dearly, Sam predicted, for no other reason than she'd taken her money from whence came their...*livelihoods.*

A shiver coursed through her.

"Are you cold, Miss Moira?" Anthony had been given leave to use her first name, although his mother insisted upon a semblance of formality. Now he tailed them and had obviously witnessed her reaction to Sam's foresight. "Seems to me it's rather hot and stuffy down here."

"No, no…I'm not cold at all. In fact, I rather agree with your assessment of the stale air."

"We'll open the port window at the saloon," Rachel said, leading the way down the dimly lit companionway. The only source of light came from the open hatch above. "Of course, it's not much of a saloon, I'm afraid."

"I wouldn't know the difference."

Rachel led her into what appeared to be a community room, with a long plank table running down the center. Four small cabins and one larger one opened from off its circumference. "Quite often the crew makes use of this room, with their chess games and rum-drinking, and such. But when we have passengers aboard, the men keep to the steerage area."

"I see."

Rachel lit a lamp then whirled around. "If I recollect, Sam said you'd once sailed before."

"Yes, but I was in a state of shock, or so a doctor has told me." Moira hugged herself. "I remember very little about the voyage. Then one day I awoke in a chamber in my uncle's home upon a padded mattress, surrounded by pretty papered walls. I had no idea how I'd gotten there. That was last September."

Rachel pulled her close. "How tragic about your parents and your conniving relatives. But, thankfully, you now have Sam."

"Yes, thankfully." Another pinch of conscience.

Rachel's smile rivaled the lamplight. "I'm still trying to figure out how you and Sam ended up marrying."

"A very long story." And one Moira didn't wish to tell. Better to allow Sam to devise the tale.

"Sam said the same thing. I would enjoy hearing it

someday."

"Perhaps someday you will."

Rachel strode to a door at the end of the saloon and opened it. "Here's your new cabin. I suggest giving it a good scrubbing before you move in. Anthony and I will help."

"No need." Moira pushed up the sleeves of her dark-green gown. "I'm happy to do all the scrubbing. It makes me feel useful."

"Well, I do have chores in the galley..."

"Then you should see to those and leave the cabin scrubbing to me."

"Very well." Rachel lit another lamp. "I shall have Anthony bring in the supplies." With that, she left, making her way through the saloon to the companionway.

Moira glanced around. The cabin was, indeed, larger than the one she and Sam presently occupied, but the fact that they were to continue sharing one was disappointing. Sam's snoring practically shook the rafters and he complained that she moaned, groaned, and mumbled in her sleep.

Actually, it wasn't so much a complaint as it was an expression of concern and Moira was forced to admit to having occasional nightmares. Sometimes it seemed they wanted to suck her into the dark, distorted underworld from whence they'd come, and she had to struggle to stay among the living. When she awoke, her hair and bedclothes were damp from the imagined tussle.

Moira clutched the silver cross that hung around her neck and pulled her thoughts back to the present. She took to exploring the other cabins and wondered if Sam would mind sleeping in one of them. She would even give him the choice of the larger of the cabins. Perhaps she'd scrub another one up too, just in case.

Anthony brought in a pail filled with soapy water, a mop, and a rag. Moira got to work. She scrubbed every nook and cranny and by the time she was finished the wood gleamed and a pleasant smell of the lemony oil she'd used on the furniture floated into the saloon. Setting down the pail, she debated whether to scrub another cabin as a favor to the Harneys. Some time later, the captain sauntered in with Rachel on his heels.

"Mrs. Stryker," he began, his hands folded behind his back, "I wonder if you might know the reason for your husband's tardiness. He should have been back long ago."

"I haven't a clue." Wild thoughts scampered across her mind. A drink somewhere? A large-bosomed serving wench on his lap? Not likely, knowing what she did of Sam. But what if he behaved as wretchedly as Uncle Tyrus and Major Nettles? He did, after all, know details of their wrongdoings.

Captain Harney came forward and put his hands on Moira's shoulders. "Now, now, don't frown so hard, my dear. I'm sure no harm has come to him. We'll wait an hour more, but that's all I can spare."

Moira forced the corners of her mouth to form a smile. "What if he doesn't show up in an hour? What if something's happened to him?"

"I've got a man on shore who is looking for him." Captain Harney let his hands drop to his sides. "But methinks, knowing Sam as I do, he most likely got…distracted inside the nearest pub."

He snorted a laugh and Rachel gave his shoulder a shove. A mask of seriousness fell over his weathered features. "He'll turn up, Mrs. Stryker. Don't you worry."

The couple left the saloon, leaving Moira with her thoughts. So her wild ideas hadn't been so wild after all. Was

Sam Stryker a womanizing rake? Moira supposed most men were—except Papa. He was ever devoted to Mum.

Moira lowered herself onto a nearby bench and wondered why she should even care if Sam was a lady's man or not. What business was it of hers? Sam was a handsome, unattached male. A spy for the American Colonies. Once they reached the shores of the United States, Moira would be on her own. She'd been searching her mind for a position she might look for, preferably as a governess or teacher...or a shopkeeper's assistant as she was quite capable with figures. Suffice it to say, Sam's bargain with her had its limits.

Anthony burst into the room, giving Moira a start.

"Mr. Sam's on his way to the ship right now and he's bringing a woman with him."

"A woman?"

"Looks like she's got brown hair, but I didn't get a close enough look."

Brown, black, what did it matter? "Thank you, Anthony."

The boy took off and Moira's heart dropped to her knees. Obviously, Sam decided to tell the Harneys the truth. Feelings of shame plumed inside of her. She'd lied to the Harneys just the same as Sam did. She was equally as guilty and stood to lose both Rachel's friendship and trust. And Sam? He obviously hadn't given Moira a second thought.

But had she really believed he would? A daisy. One in a million in the meadow of life. That's all she was. Nothing special.

Then why did she feel as glum as the day Uncle Tyrus announced she was betrothed to Major Nettles?

Moira carried the pail and mop up to the first mate's cabin. She packed Sam's things into his sea chest and then folded her meager articles of clothing into her valise. She caught the attention of a passing crewman and asked if their belongings could be taken to the saloon. The crewman was kind enough to take up the matter himself. He swung Sam's chest up and onto one broad shoulder. Moira kept her valise with her. She then set to the task of scrubbing the cabin. About halfway through, Mr. Jamison, the first mate, showed up. His bushy eyebrows shot up when he glimpsed Moira on her knees, scrub brush in hand.

"I'll be finished in a few minutes."

"Ye don' have to be cleaning my cabin, Missus." He came forward and hauled Moira to her feet.

"I only meant to repay your kindness of allowing Sam and me to make use of it."

"Not necessary, ma'am. I didn't have much choice in the matter." His voice lacked inflection. "You go on, now. I'll finish up here."

With a hand on her shoulder blade he walked her—pushed her, actually—to the door. Moira barely had a chance to grab her valise before the cabin door closed behind her with a decided bang.

She stared at the wooden door, wondering if the truth was out now and the Harneys as well as the crew of the *Seahawk* knew she was nothing more than a liar. Perchance they thought her a loose woman. After all, she'd shared a cabin with a man who wasn't her husband. Nothing romantic had happened between Sam and her, but the crew didn't know that.

Moira's throat constricted with raw emotion and she decided she'd disembark here in Portugal. She had her possessions in hand and her money on her person. How could she bear another four or five weeks aboard a ship where her reputation was thoroughly ruined?

Slowly, Moira made her way down the companionway,

toward the hatch. She climbed the steps, thankful that the sea wind quickly dried the tears that had gathered in her eyes. She blinked and looked about for the captain.

"There you are!"

Sam's voice swung her around.

"I've been looking everywhere for you." His blue eyes snapped with something akin to excitement. "I've brought aboard someone I want you to meet."

"No thank you." The last thing she wanted was to meet his new...companion. "But I do wonder what you've told the Harneys."

A frown creased his forehead.

"Never mind. I probably shan't see them ever again. I'm disembarking here—if the captain will allow it, of course. I think it's for the best, at least for me."

"You want to get off?" Sam's palm wrapped around her elbow and he pulled her closer and out of the way of crewmen who'd begun scurrying about. "We're pulling up anchor right now."

"Then I'd best hurry." She pulled free, intending to find the captain.

"Moira, what's happened?" Sam reclaimed her elbow and stood mere inches away. He reeked of tobacco and ale. "Tell me."

"What's happened?" She narrowed her gaze. "Why, you should know better than anyone. You've brought a serving wench aboard to...entertain you. Everyone now knows we're liars, and I can't bear the shame of it." She turned her face to the wind again. She wouldn't allow him to see the inexplicable sadness she felt. "I care not that Portugal is but a couple of weeks' journey from England. I refuse to stay aboard under the present circumstances."

"A serving wench?" Sam hung his head back and laughed so hard, the sound shook the deck on which they stood. "Are you jealous, my darling daisy?" Amusement danced in his eyes.

"How dare you ask such a thing!" She twisted out of his grasp and darted toward Captain Harney, who barked orders to his crewmen.

Sam's arm snaked around her waist and in seconds she was whirled around toward the hatch and all but carried down the stairs. Somewhere she dropped her valise.

"Unhand me, sir."

Sam's arm clenched tighter and his lips touched her ear. "Take care what you say."

There was a dangerous edge in his tone that sobered Moira.

"Now, start walking toward the saloon without complaint and a smile on your face. Understand?"

She nodded, both amazed and terrified. Despite his charm and good manners, Sam was still the man who'd threatened to kill her—to drown her, if need be.

At the moment, she was certain he would do the latter if she didn't comply.

She made quick steps to the saloon, nodding politely to the sailors she passed by.

Once inside the cabin she'd scrubbed, Sam slammed the door closed behind them. She spun on her heel to face him. Sam set down her valise and then shrugged out of his frockcoat. "This cabin smells a far sight better than any I've ever had the pleasure of occupying."

Moira said nothing.

"I understand you've been cleaning today."

She gave a nod when he glanced her way.

"Now, I am curious…" He folded his arms over his broad

chest. "How on earth did you come up with the idea that I brought a serving wench on board?"

Moira explained how Captain Harney had mentioned Sam's tardiness and suspected he'd frequented a pub and lost track of time. She told of Anthony's exclamation of Sam bringing a woman on board with him—a woman with brown hair.

"I appreciate your giving me the benefit of the doubt." Sarcasm dripped off his every word. "And now I'd like you to meet this...*woman with brown hair.*"

Sam opened the door and indicated she should follow. At the smaller of the two cabins off the saloon, Sam knocked on the door. The male voice bid them enter, and Sam turned the knob. The entryway soon revealed a short man wearing a brown, hooded robe.

"Moira, my darling daisy..."

Each word felt like a punch in her midsection as she stared at the new passenger.

"I'd like you to meet Brother Tobias."

The man pushed the hood off his head, revealing a shiny, bald head. "A pleasure to meet you, madam."

Chapter Ten

.... ⌒♥⌒ ....

"He seems like a nice enough fellow."

"A monk who left his monastery to sail for America with the intention of teaching school and ministering to *the savages*, as he calls the people of the First Nation." Sam heaved a sigh. "He has much to learn about the Native Americans before he can reach them for the Almighty, that's for sure."

"But a worthy undertaking, nonetheless." Moira's pride lay in shreds. Obviously Anthony had mistaken Brother Tobias's brown hood for hair when he'd seen him in the distance. He recognized Sam, but not his...*guest.*

And Moira had assumed the worst.

She met Sam's stare. He leaned against the closed cabin door, arms still folded, his booted feet crossed. Obviously he was waiting for an apology.

And he deserved one.

"I'm sorry I behaved so impulsively." She dropped her gaze. "I panicked."

Moments of silence passed, seeming like hours.

"Do you really believe that I'd jeopardize my mission and your escape by bringing a serving wench, of all creatures, aboard this ship?"

She peeked at him. "This morning I'd have emphatically said no. But earlier, when Captain Harney guessed at the reason for your tardiness, I figured he knew you better than I did."

"And now?"

"Now..." Moira's emotions seemed tangled in knots. However, she knew she'd been wrong to have reckoned the worst. "I should not have jumped to conclusions."

Sam grunted in reply and continued his hard stare. "I hoped to hear that you trust me."

"I would have rather proved that I did in this situation." She shrugged. "Not much of a spy, am I?"

A slight grin cracked his stony façade. "You're the worst spy ever."

Tears threatened, but she blinked them away.

"You're kind, caring, and terribly honest."

Moira frowned. "You make those attributes sound like faults."

"In a spy's world, they are."

She rolled a shoulder as if she couldn't care less.

"Now I'd like to hear from your lips three words that describe me."

Moira lifted her chin and gave his request several moments' thought.

Sam arched a brow. "A man deserves to know where he stands."

"All right, then." She pulled back her shoulders. "You're gentlemanly, respectful, and terribly charming." With the latter she mocked him, but regretted it almost at once. If not for Sam, she'd be readying herself for marriage to Major Joseph Nettles.

"I would like to add gallant and trustworthy to my description of you, though that's five words not three." She met his gaze, hoping he saw the sincerity she felt. "Gallant because you rescued me from a fate worse than death and trustworthy as you've not given me a reason to distrust you. I realize that now…now that I'm thinking rationally again. You're right. I should have given you the benefit of the doubt."

"I don't sound like much of a spy either, do I?" His stoic features gave way to a grin.

Moira stepped toward him. "So…you forgive me?"

"Of course. And let us put this matter behind us."

"Agreed." Relief pumped through her veins with each beat of her heart.

"I brought you gifts from the market." Sam lifted a short stack of colorful folded fabric from off his sea chest. Moira hadn't noticed it there until now. He placed it in her arms. "I took it upon myself to purchase materials for new gowns. It's my fault you didn't have time to sufficiently pack, and I've grown tired of seeing *my wife* in drab Puritan garb."

Moira looked down at the dark-green gown she wore. She'd stuffed it and a brown one of similar style in her valise. Both garments had been given to her by someone, and she knew nothing of that person's identity. To cover the low neckline, she habitually buttoned on the crocheted collar she'd made. Aunt Aggie had promised Moira a shopping expedition upon her betrothal to Major Nettles as if that somehow made the match more tolerable. But the trip into London never happened. The only new gown Moira acquired was the one she wore the night of her engagement party, and Aunt Aggie had selected it.

"Has my attire been that horrid?"

"I shall answer that question by stating you deserve far better." Sam shook out one of the folded fabrics and the sunny yellow, pink, and gray print cheered the darkly-paneled cabin. "I can envision you wearing a gown of this material." He held it to her chin and stepped back. "What do you think? Do you like it?"

"It's lovely."

He arched a brow as he folded the fabric. "You do know how to sew, don't you?"

"Of course. Up until my parents perished, I made all my clothes."

"Good, but ask Rachel for a fashionable pattern."

"All right." His insult, whether intended or not, stung. Even so, Sam's observation of her rather dowdy wardrobe caused her to see it in a different light and, oddly, a river of enthusiasm coursed through her at the thought of new gowns. "I've never worn such a pretty fabric."

Sam's smile indicated his pleasure. He shook out the second piece of fabric. Moira almost forgot she held it. "And what say you of this print?"

Moira looked over the tiny green buds against a fawn-colored background. "I like it very much."

"The woman at the market insisted I purchase the trimmings too." He refolded the material and set in on his sea chest. "You're happy then?"

"Very happy." She meant each word. "Thank you, Sam."

"You deserve it." He crossed the cabin and put his palms on her shoulders. "I believe your family served the Almighty sacrificially and then you witnessed more horror than any young lady ought to. Pretty fabric is the least you should have."

Moira swallowed the sudden lump of emotion that wedged

in her throat. "I don't want your pity, Sam."

"Good, because I've no pity to give."

A smile tugged at her lips. "And here I thought the worst of you while you thought the best of me and even purchased beautiful fabrics for me." She lowered her chin and stared at the tips of her leather booties.

Sam stepped back. "I thought we agreed to move past that matter."

She bobbed her head. "We did, indeed."

"Then I'd prefer a smile to a frown." He glanced at his pocket watch. "Shall we ready ourselves for dinner? Brother Tobias will be joining us and he enjoys talking."

"As I understand it," Moira put in quickly, glad to have a subject change, "some monks are not allowed to speak at the monastery."

"Quite true, my darling daisy, and with my skill of extracting information, Brother Tobias shall be blabbing secrets, valuable to the United States, within an hour."

"Do you think he knows any…secrets?"

"Perchance he's heard some confessions." A rather devilish gleam sparked in Sam's blue eyes.

Moira thought that a fair possibility. "Perchance he has."

Sam placed his hands on his hips. "In either case, I intend to find out."

••••ᘒᔆ♥ᔆᘒ••••

"Remember what I told you." Sam spoke so close to Moira's neck that his warm breath tickled.

Smiling, she gave Sam a nod then continued to watch the goings-on. Sailors ran to and fro while the captain shouted orders. Men climbed high on ratlines, each doing his part to secure the sails. Somehow Rachel had convinced the captain to drop anchor and give them a day to enjoy dry land before they caught the trade winds.

And now Moira waited her turn to descend to the long narrow boat bobbing alongside the ship.

"Anthony will climb down the ladder first." Sam's breath tickled her neck. "Watch how he does it."

The boy proved no help; he descended in record time. Rachel followed.

Moira pivoted around. "Sam, I don't think…"

"Your turn." His expression told her he'd not allow her to get out of it.

Just as Rachel had demonstrated, Moira tied her skirts to ensure a semblance of modesty.

"Come on, Moira." Rachel lifted a hand and beckoned to her from a plank seat on the boat below. "You can do it."

Sam gave her a nod of encouragement and she swung her left leg over the side of the ship. He assisted her until she'd gotten a secure hold of the ropes.

As it happened, going down the ladder proved much easier than climbing up. Within minutes she dropped onto the plank bench across from Rachel and Anthony. Only seconds later, it seemed, Sam sat beside her. Moments more passed and then Captain Harney joined them, having left Mr. Jamison in charge aboard the *Seahawk*. Soon they were headed ashore. Beneath their feet lay paraphernalia for tent building and fire making, and Moira couldn't help but catch the excitement of the impending holiday on a sandy beach.

Reaching the shoreline of what appeared to be an otherwise deserted island, they disembarked. The men made quick work of pitching the tent and hanging a large iron kettle a safe way off. It would do nicely for boiling the day's catch. Then, while the men left to do their fishing, Rachel and Moira removed their shoes and stockings and gathered dried wood for their fire.

"It's a shame that Brother Tobias couldn't join us last night," Rachel said, depositing an armful of kindling on the growing pile. "And this morning he said he did not feel up to a day on the beach."

"I don't mind saying I'm a bit concerned for him," Moira admitted. "Last night he had a pounding headache and today he looked feverish. However, he wouldn't allow me to come into his cabin to help, insisting whatever ailed him might be contagious."

Frown lines appeared on Rachel's forehead. "I pray it is not. The last thing I need is a crew of sick men."

"Perish the thought!" Moira wondered if they'd ever reach the United States if that should occur.

"I shall do that, my new friend, leastwise for today."

Soon a fire burned and the kettle sat ready beside it. Before long, Captain Harney, Anthony, and Sam returned with a string of fish for roasting.

"No crab?" Rachel put her hands on her curvy hips and pouted.

"Now, now, my dear…" Her husband slung one arm around her shoulders. "The fish are biting and the crabs are hiding. 'Tis the nature of it, I'm afraid."

Sam rubbed his palms together. "May as well enjoy fresh fish today, because in a few weeks we'll be awfully tired of beans."

Rachel gave a toss of her head. "Not the way I make them, you won't be."

"Ah, I stand corrected." Sam gave formal bow and Moira swallowed a giggle.

She sat back, her arms supporting her, and wiggled her

toes in the warm sand. As long as Rachel didn't view it as improper to be barefoot in the presence of men, Moira couldn't see any harm in it. The skirt of her gown covered her legs. At the village in Uganda, she went without shoes and stockings quite often when playing with the children. Papa often said that subtle conformities to a particular culture, conformities that didn't violate God's commandments, were often a step toward acceptance by that culture.

Sam plopped down right beside her. He sat mere inches away. He, too, had removed his stockings and boots and the ends of his breeches were rolled above his knees, revealing well-developed calves. Obviously he had no need to stuff sandbags into his stockings the way some men did.

Men, perhaps, like Major Nettles. A grin worked its way across her lips.

"What amuses you, my darling daisy?" Sam whispered, leaning closer.

"Sandbags."

"What's so funny about sandbags?"

Moira giggled again, although she didn't move away. Oddly, she'd grown accustomed to his nearness. Moreover, he'd become one of the best friends she'd ever known. Moving around as she and her parents did, Moira hadn't time to make close acquaintances. But as close as she felt to Sam, she couldn't get herself to reveal exactly what she'd found so funny. *Major Nettles in sandbags.*

She laughed inwardly and gave Sam a smile. "I'm enjoying my holiday. Aren't you?"

"I am, indeed. And I'll have you know that I caught the biggest fish."

"Did you?"

"And the most, too." He winked, indicating his joke.

"I heard that, you devil!" Captain Harney scowled at Sam, although it lacked its usual fierceness. "I caught the largest fish."

"Did not," said Anthony. "I did."

"Now why am I apt to believe the boy?" With one dark eyebrow arched, Rachel looked from her husband to Sam while unpacking two loaves of bread.

"You believe me, Mama, cuz I don't tell fish tales the way some sailors do."

The captain guffawed and Sam chuckled.

"Aye." Rachel sent a glance to the heavens.

The banter continued during the fish-roasting, feasting, and over the course of the next couple hours. A peace settled around Moira. She couldn't recall the last time she enjoyed relaxing.

Sam grabbed hold of her wrist and pulled her to her feet. She opened her mouth to ask what he planned when he made the announcement.

"It's time you learned to swim."

"What?" She attempted to tug her wrist from his grasp, but Sam held on tightly and led her toward the water. "Learn to swim? I should say not!"

Anthony was beside her in seconds. "It's easy, Miss Moira." He jogged to catch up with Sam. "Can I show her how, Mr. Stryker?"

"You sure can. You'll be my demonstrator."

Anthony's grin reflected his joy.

But Moira had no wish to be the student. "Sam, no."

He switched hands, never releasing her wrist, and placed his arm around her waist. "I'm going to teach you how to float on your back. That way, you'll never fear the water again, because you'll know how to survive until help comes."

"Please, Sam, no." She dug her heels into the sand. "I have nightmares about drowning."

"Yes, I'm aware of them." His gaze locked on hers. "You talk in your sleep."

Moira gasped. "Do I?"

At Sam's nod, Moira's face grew warm, and not from the sun blazing down on them.

"We won't go into deep water, and I'll stay right beside you."

"Well…"

"A simple back float."

"Look at me, Miss Moira!" Anthony lay on his back, albeit only his head was visible. "It's easy."

Sam stretched out his hand toward the boy. "Out of the mouths of babes."

"I suppose I could give it at least one try."

"That's my girl."

At that very moment, Moira wished it was so—that she belonged to Sam.

But it was not to be. He made that clear.

They waded out until the water came to their hips. Moira's skirt billowed and she back-stepped to shallower water and tied her hems like she'd done to descend the rope ladder. Then she walked out to Sam. She felt the ripple of the ocean floor beneath her feet.

Sam stood at her right and placed his hand on the back of her neck. "Allow yourself to fall backwards. I'll hold you."

She hesitated.

"Trust me."

She gave it a moment's thought. "I do trust you, Sam."

"Good. I'll not give you a reason to distrust me, I swear."

Anthony floated by on his back as if to encourage her.

Moira followed Sam's directions and let herself fall backwards. As promised, Sam held her as the water inched over her until she was submerged to her chin. Water filled her ears. Her breath caught.

"Relax. I've got you," came Sam's muffled voice. "Breathe normally."

Breathe. She fought against the rising panic. *Breathe.* She gazed up at the flyaway-blue sky. Suddenly it was Sam's lapis-colored eyes she saw as he gazed down at her.

"Cup your hands and make circular motions, but take care not to splash."

Moira did as instructed and, oddly, concentrating on the hand movements slowed her breathing.

"You're floating!" Anthony's voice sounded dim, but still infused with excitement. You're floating, Miss Moira!"

A moment later she glimpsed Sam, standing beside Anthony. They smiled and waved. No one was holding her. She was on the water by herself.

I have you in the palm of my hand, Beloved. God's promise filled her heart. *Not a sparrow falls...never be afraid, for you are far more valuable than sparrows.*

A wave splashed over her, but Moira kept floating. Anthony continued to cheer her on. The water cooled her skin beneath the sun's scorching rays and she began to find floating quite relaxing.

She startled when Sam popped up from beneath the ocean's surface. The water seemed to suck her under and she breathed in salt water. Her lungs convulsed. Panic consumed her until a pair of strong hands righted her. Her feet found the sandy ocean bottom, but the coughing continued as she struggled for a breath.

She heard Sam apologize and reached for him. Her

fingertips found the fabric of his wet shirt and she grabbed hold of it, praying he'd help her somehow. As if she'd spoken aloud, he clapped her between the shoulder blades a few times and, at last, she rid her lungs of seawater.

She sagged against him.

"I'm sorry, Moira." He kissed the top of her head. "I meant to surprise you, not drown you."

Words escaped her.

"But you did quite well with your first floating lesson. You floated like a seasoned sailor."

"Seasoned sailor?" She grinned in spite of herself and stepped back, although her retort was lost by the crewman rowing toward them with determined strokes and a frown weighing his features.

"Where's the captain?" The man pulled up the oars long enough for Sam to reply.

"What do you suppose is wrong?" Moira turned to Sam, who took her hand and called to Anthony.

The three of them headed for shore and trudged over the hot sand. When they reached the captain, Rachel, and the crewman, all expressions were glum. Moira shivered as the water dripped from her every pore.

"A British warship is headed straight for us." Captain Harney removed his cap and finger-combed his dark hair from off his forehead before slapping his cap back on. "Four hours and she'll be on top of us." He glanced around. "We must pack up and get back onboard, posthaste!"

Chapter Eleven

"Cap'n!" a crewman called. "They're sendin' a light signal."

"Can you decipher it, Mr. Simmons?" Harney shielded his eyes and glanced at the lookout.

"Aye, sir. I'll do m' best."

A feeling of helplessness engulfed Sam and he clenched his fists. He needed to do something other than stand here like a column of coiled rope. He watched while Harney lifted his spyglass and aimed toward the warship that had trailed the *Seahawk* all afternoon. Although both ships flew the Union Jack, the frigate obviously suspected something amiss onboard Harney's vessel.

As if divining his thoughts, Moira clutched his arm. Sam covered her hand with his. "We don't know they're after us." He meant his words for her ears only. "Could be they learned Harney is taking supplies to the colonies and they intend to stop him."

Her silence spoke volumes. She didn't believe a word he'd just spoken.

Neither did he.

"It's somethin' 'bout a kidnapping," Mr. Simmons hollered

to the captain as the light continued to blink from the warship, sending the remaining message. "Kidnapping a woman. The Brits think she and her abductor may be aboard the *Seahawk* and they're demanding we turn them both over."

Moira gasped.

The crewman turned to face Harney. "They're wantin' to send sailors to board the *Seahawk* to fetch them."

"Mr. Stryker!" Harney swiveled around. "Might you know anything about this…kidnapping?"

"No, sir."

"I went willingly with Sam," Moira blurted.

Sam grudgingly gave up a nod. . "That's the truth, Captain."

"I'll see you both in my quarters. Now!" Before departing below, Harney barked orders to his crew.

Sam led Moira to the hatch and then down the companionway. At their knock on the captain's door, Rachel answered and bid them enter.

Harney followed within a minute. "Stryker, what in the world is going on?"

He held out his hands. "There's been no kidnapping."

"Kidnapping?" Rachel put her hands on her hips and looked from him to Moira.

"I was to marry a horrid man, but Sam rescued me." Moira folded her arm around his. "I went willingly and I left a note for my aunt and uncle, telling them not to worry."

"You left a note?" Sam didn't know that.

"A brief one." She stared up into his eyes. "I mentioned no names."

Harney groaned. "I trust you have the proper marital papers on you, Sam?"

"No time for papers, I'm afraid."

Moira hid her face against his shoulder, but the challenge in Harney's eyes worried Sam more than his wrath.

"I have the perfect solution." Harney snapped his fingers and grinned. "I'm master and commander of this ship, ordained for funerals and..." He leaned forward on his desk. "And anything else that arises. Like marriages. I'll wed you both right now and give you the appropriate documents. Rachel can stand as a witness."

If Harney expected an objection, Sam would give him none. Obviously his friend called his bluff, most likely suspecting that Sam lied about his relationship with Moira. Which was true. But Sam wasn't about to turn her over to the British, nor would he turn himself in.

Would Moira understand?

He sank his gaze into her smoky eyes. The sun had kissed her skin this afternoon, giving her a golden glow. She gave him a tentative smile. Yes, she knew this officiating was mere playacting. After all, he'd stated on more than one occasion that he'd never marry.

Then why, of late, did he imagine an emptier life once he and Moira parted? It was rather nice, returning to the cabin at night and listening to her soft and steady breathing as she slept. Yes, he'd heard her cry out during nightmares. She'd admitted to dreams of drowning and of her parents' deaths. She'd faced much tragedy in her young life and Sam refused to add to it. Rather, he wished to help, thus the floating lesson today, which went a bit awry. Still, she'd experienced mild success and looked no worse for wear.

"Well, what say you, Sam? Should we get on with it then?"

"Absolutely. It will solve any issues should the *Seahawk* be boarded by the British."

Harney snorted. "Perish the thought. They'll hang us both,

abuse our women, kill our crew—after they impress the better of them."

Moira gasped.

Rachel hugged herself and shuddered.

Sam set his palm over Moira's hand, still wrapped around his elbow. "But we'll not let that happen, will we, Captain Harney?"

"By God, I should say not!" The older man looked about. "Everyone ready for the ceremony?" Harney didn't wait for responses. "Good." He opened the Bible. "This is God's word and contains God's commandments. Do you both swear to keep them?"

"I swear."

"I swear." Moira's voice sounded stronger, surer, than he expected.

"Sam, do you promise to be a good husband and leave your sinful bachelorhood behind?"

He arched a brow. "That's not how it goes, Harney."

"That's how it goes on my ship. Now do you promise this young lady or don't you?"

"I promise."

"Look at your bride when you speak your vows."

Sam did as his friend bid him. "I promise."

Questions, or perhaps it was doubt, pooled in her gray gaze—and with good reason.

"Miss Moira, do you promise to leave your maidenhood behind for this rambling, no-account American spy who has undoubtedly clouded your good judgment with his charm and boyish good looks?"

Rachel laughed softly.

Sam bristled. "Harney, for pity's sake!"

"I promise." Moira replied as if this affair was a formal

one. Her eyes darkened with obvious sincerity. "I, Moira Kingsley, take thee, Samuel Stryker, to have and to hold, from this day forward, for better, for worse, for richer, for poorer, in sickness and in health, to love and to cherish, till death do us part, according to God's holy ordinance; and thereto I give thee mine heart and pledge thee my troth."

Sam sent Harney a good-natured smirk. "*That's* how it goes." But one glimpse at Moira and Sam knew she'd meant every word.

Annoyance dropped like an anchor inside of him. He shifted from one foot to another. Didn't she understand that this was a mock ceremony? A farce, as untrue as their fibs. Once on U. S. soil Sam planned to have this marriage, as it were, annulled.

"Very well," Harney growled. "I now pronounce you husband and wife." He seated himself at his desk and fished a paper from a drawer.

"Aren't you going to say I can kiss my bride?" Sam couldn't help the jab.

"Go ahead. Kiss her."

Sam ignored Moira's wide-eyed gaze and cupped her face. With the utmost deliberation, he brushed his lips against hers. She didn't withdraw, but leaned into him, and Sam deepened their kiss. She smelled like a fresh ocean breeze. His senses tumbled into a whirlpool of desire as he trailed kisses along her smooth jaw line…

"All right, you two, time to make this marriage official."

Harney's voice broke the spell, although Moira looked a bit dazed, causing Sam to grin.

Harney scratched his name across the bottom of the document then turned it over to Sam, who did likewise. Moira neatly penned her name next and Rachel made her mark, verifying that she'd witnessed the occasion. Harney recorded the marriage in his captain's log then slammed the volume closed. "Now to take care of a certain British warship."

Rachel snagged Moira's arm. "Perhaps you'd stay and help me tend to Brother Tobias. He's quite ill, the poor man."

"Yes, of course." Moira turned to Sam with arched eyebrows.

He gave a nod before following Harney aloft. A flurry of activity greeted them.

"Cap'n, the Brits are insisting on sending a few men to board the *Seahawk* now," Mr. Jamison, the first mate announced. "How shall we reply?"

"Tell them to send their first mate and an officer. We'll give them our usual welcome."

"The usual welcome, lads," Jamison shouted and the instruction was repeated on down through the ranks.

"Harney, you can't be serious." Sam stepped in beside the captain, a man he considered to be a friend—more friend than foe, anyway. "You said yourself that the Brits will hang us."

"Do not question my judgment, Mr. Stryker. This is my ship and I'm in command."

"Yes, sir." Sam couldn't keep the sarcasm from his voice. He clenched his jaw, searching his mind for a solution of his own. He looked toward the beach where they'd spent an enjoyable few hours and supposed he could swim for it. The island, however, appeared abandoned like his mission would have to be, should he either be caught or become a castaway.

He thought on it some more. He'd learned survival skills from his mother's people, the Catawba, but what of Moira? He could hardly ask her to jump ship with him.

"Why don't you trust your captain, Stryker, instead of standing there plotting against him?"

Sam put his hands on his hips. "You're accusing me of mutiny?"

"I'm accusing you of distrusting your friends." Harney lifted his chin and met Sam's stare. "Relax, Stryker. I've got this situation handled. Trust me."

"All right. You've never given me reason to distrust you…yet."

Half of Harney's mouth curved upward, part sneer and part grin. "You will be expected to take up arms against the British if it should come to that…which it won't."

"Understood."

"Boat's in the water, Cap'n," the lookout called. "Two men aboard."

Harney retrieved his spyglass, looked, then handed it to Sam. "Recognize either man?"

Sam peered at the two, one ensconced in blue and the other in an infamous red jacket. A second later, Joseph Nettles's arrogant face came into focus.

"I know one of them. The redcoat. He's the man from whom Moira is trying to escape." Sam relayed all pertinent information.

"After her inheritance, is he?" Harney chuckled. "Aye, men will go far if money is involved. Just how far, is the question."

"He's followed her this far."

"Hmm…and how fortunate for you that you've wed a wealthy young lady."

"Moira's money holds no interest for me."

"Until you lose your first card game." Harney snorted, looking amused.

"I'm glad you think so highly of me…*friend*."

Harney stepped closer to Sam. "My wife is a good woman

and she is quite fond of your wife. Rachel says she's sweet and all goodness. A missionary's daughter who has experienced her share of heartbreak."

"All true."

Harney's gaze darkened. "We'd hate to see her get hurt."

So that was it. Sam bit down hard, till the muscles in his jaw ached. "Moira knows what she's gotten herself into."

Harney puffed out his lower lip, shrugged, then looked through his spyglass again. "Well, we've got a fine welcome in store for your wife's pursuant." A grin at Sam, and then Harney bellowed to his men. "Ready the welcome, lads!"

"Aye, Captain!" came the returns from sailors on deck and up on the ratlines. It made for an odd male chorus, followed by a flurry of activity. Sails dropped and caught the wind.

"What's the 'usual welcome'?"

"It's a trick my men and I enjoy playing on hostile sailors, like the Brits." Harney glanced over his shoulder at Sam. "We act like we're waiting for them to board, see? But before they reach us, we pull up anchor…well, just pay attention and you'll understand soon enough." He trained his spyglass on the Brits in the rowboat.

"Now, Cap'n?" Jamison asked.

"Not yet. Easy, let them get a little closer. Closer…"

Sam could make out Nettles's identity without the spyglass now.

Harney suddenly made the call and the sailors pulled up the anchor. The *Seahawk* began to move toward the front of the warship to avoid cannon fire. The men in the narrow boat obviously realized a trick had been played and began rowing vigorously back toward the warship amid Nettles's shouts. A cannon fired, whizzing over the heads of the men in the rowboat. The lead ball dropped into the water with a heavy splash.

Then Nettles did the unthinkable. He stood up in the rowboat. Sam straightened. Even he, unskilled in the way of ships and navigations, knew not to stand in a rowboat unless boarding a larger ship. It put a man in danger of tumbling overboard.

Nettles shook his fist at the *Seahawk* and shouted obscenities. The long, narrow boat seesawed in the choppy water. Moments later, as Sam predicted, a wave toppled Nettles into the ocean, giving Harney and his crew a good laugh and earning well-deserved mockery.

A moment later, Harney returned to shouting orders. His first mate, Jamison, repeated them and the shouting went on down the ranks.

"Doesn't look like that soldier is surfacing, Cap'n," a sailor shouted from high on the rigging.

Sam moved to the starboard side and peered across the distance. The sailor in the rowboat circled the area, peering into the deep. Only moments later, thrashing a good ways off caught Sam's attention.

"There!" He pointed toward the west. "There he is."

Harney squinted into the sun. "Sure enough." He trained his spyglass on the bobbing redcoat. "The current is strong and pulling him farther out to sea. Doesn't appear the man can swim. Doubtful that a fellow crewman will reach him in time."

Sam turned away. While he couldn't rightly say he was sorry to see Nettles drown. The man was a scoundrel at best and, no doubt, harbored evil plans for Moira, had he caught her. He'd scarred a serving wench for mere fun. Imagine what he might do with his sword if his wrath had gotten the better of him?

Even so, he took no joy in watching a man die.

Inhaling deeply, Sam looked back and Nettles sank beneath the water again and this time, he didn't resurface.

Sam met Harney's gaze.

"Your wife will not have to worry about that man again, Mr. Stryker."

"'Twill be a relief, to be sure."

Sails clapped above and gave in to the wind. The *Seahawk* picked up speed. The warship would be late in its pursuit, having to wait for the lone sailor to re-board.

Sam released a long sigh. They were safe...at least for now.

Chapter Twelve

"I have news."

Moira glanced up from the herbs she soaked according to Rachel's instructions. By God's grace, these herbs would ease Brother Tobias's fever. "What news would that be?"

Sam leaned against the opening of the galley and folded his arms across his broad chest. The sun had tanned his face and his exposed forearms today, as he'd rolled his shirt's sleeves to his elbows. He most certainly made for a pleasant eyeful. "Major Nettles has drowned."

Moira froze. "Drowned? How do you know?"

"I saw him stand in the rowboat, his fist in the air, cursing us to the deeps, and then he fell overboard."

Moira gasped and pressed her fingers to her lips.

"Evidently, the man couldn't swim." Sam's blue eyes twinkled. "Couldn't even float on his back until help arrived—unlike you, who now knows what to do if such a calamity befalls."

"I am relieved—although I should be saddened to learn a soul has perished."

"I, too, found it difficult to watch helplessly as a man

102

drowned, but Nettles acted foolishly and bore the consequences of it."

Moira felt rather breathless and realized she'd been hoarding an inhale. "I wish death on no man, not even him...not even on the enemy tribesmen who murdered my parents. Even so, I'd be a liar if I claimed to mourn Nettles's loss of life."

"I see it as a blessing, for now I don't have to kill him."

Moira tipped her head and felt the weight of the frown on her brow. "You planned to kill Major Nettles?"

"I didn't plan it, darling daisy, but it would have likely come to it if we'd met face to face." Sam arched a brow and his gaze darkened. "Be assured, Nettles most likely plotted and planned not only my demise but yours as well."

Sam spoke the truth and the reality of it had a dizzying effect on her. So much so, she stated the obvious. "Nettles was on that British warship, following us?"

"Yes. And he was in the process of being ferried from the frigate to the *Seahawk* when he made the unwise choice of standing in the rowboat."

Moira frowned. "Captain Harney would have allowed them to come aboard?"

"Nay, it was a trick all along." Sam's chest expanded with the deep breath he took. "As it happens, Harney and his crew are well-versed at escaping British frigates. Just part of being a sailor during this bloody war." He raked his fingers through his golden-brown hair. "Suffice it to say, Harney has successfully outrun the frigate...for now."

Moira took a step toward him. "Will they continue to follow us?"

"Most likely. As you might know, the British navy has been impressing men into its service. It's the very action that sparked this war. Well, that, and the fact that we attempted to steal Canada from the Crown."

Moira had all but forgotten about England's war with the colonies. Until now it hadn't impacted her life in any way.

But here she stood, legally married to an American spy. No doubt it was time to learn everything possible about the conflict.

Lesson four of her spy schooling.

"And, um, about what occurred earlier in Harney's quarters..." Sam glanced over one shoulder then the other before inching forward. "You're aware any vows we made were in pretense."

Moira nodded. She knew they hadn't meant anything to Sam.

"I thought I'd make it plain as you seemed quite sincere when you spoke."

"I was sincere, Sam." She'd promised never to lie or deceive him, and she wouldn't. "I cannot take a vow before God in pretense."

He opened his mouth to speak, but Moira quickly placed her fingers against his mouth.

"But I know our vows mean nothing to you." She let her hand fall away. "I'm also aware that as soon as we reach the colonies, you'll file the appropriate legal documents to dissolve our...marriage."

"No one wants to see you get hurt, Moira, least of all me."

Too late for that sentiment, for somewhere deep within her she'd formed a strong attachment to Sam. He was, after all, her rescuer and protector.

"You're not to concern yourself with me." Moira turned back to the herbs for Brother Tobias's fever. "When I was sixteen and all long limbs, large teeth, and limp bark-brown hair, Papa said it was apparent that I'd remain a single woman, and he prepared me to live independently. My inheritance was set aside with the intent of supporting me until I found a respectable position within a community or joined a mission team as my parents did." She sent a glance Sam's way and noted the way his gaze sharpened and full lips became a single, narrow slash. "I'm prepared to use the money for precisely those opportunities, whichever comes first." Focusing on the herbs again, she added, "So if you'll kindly point me in the right direction once we reach our destination, I'll go my own way. You're not obligated to me." Lifting the bowl, she turned toward the entryway. "'Tis I who am obligated to you, Sam. I owe you my very life."

He shook his head, but before he could speak further on the subject, Moira slipped past him and headed for the feverish man.

She heard Sam's booted feet set off behind her, trailing her all the way into the saloon and then into Brother Tobias's cabin.

Moira set down the bowl of herbs and water.

Rachel sent a grateful look her way. "He's fevering badly." She soaked a rag, wrung it out, then placed it on Brother Tobias's forehead.

"You should not be here," the sick man croaked. "You must go at once."

"Nonsense." Rachel squared her shoulders. "You need help."

"Then help yourselves, dear ladies and Mr. Stryker…leave me be."

"Perhaps if you told us why…" Moira stood directly behind Rachel, who had seated herself on the bed.

"The orphans home…" His breathing seemed somewhat

labored. "Our monastery helped those pitiful children. They'd contracted...." He sucked in another breath. "Contracted the typhus."

Moira froze while Rachel popped up from her bedside perch. The typhus! Everyone knew it was a fatal disease.

Sam pushed his way to Brother Tobias's side. "How could you beg me to take you aboard when you knew—"

"No, sir, please believe me. I did not know I had it." He wheezed as he sucked in a breath. "Thought I'd escaped with my health intact."

"Sam." Rachel touched his forearm. "I'll need you to undress him as his robe and any other contaminated garments will have to be discarded."

He gave a nod.

"Take care and put his clothing in a sheet then toss it overboard. However, none of the crew must see you. If word gets out there's typhus on board, mutiny may result."

"Understood."

"Moira, come with me, if you please."

They traipsed back to the galley where Rachel concocted some warm drink that included a healthy dose of rum and quinine. Worry lines seemed etched into her forehead. Moira touched Rachel's forearm. "I'm not afraid to die, my friend. I'll care for the man. You have a husband and a son to look after. God knows we need our captain and little Anthony needs his mum."

Rachel whirled around. "What about you? You're young and newly married."

Except my husband didn't mean a single word of his vows. "Sam will not mind, I assure you."

"Of course he'll mind." Questions clouded Rachel's gaze. "What are you saying?"

106

"He knows my parents were missionaries and that I would rather die, being about the Lord's work than not."

"Well…"

"I shall care for Brother Tobias." Rachel's lovely dark features smoothed out. Her gaze filled with gratitude. "Whatever you need, just slip a note beneath the door."

"Thank you."

With the new herbal water prepared, Rachel filled another bowl with warm water, then added a scrub brush, a rag, and a bar of strong-smelling lye soap. "The first thing you must do is scrub that man from head to toe."

Moira's face felt as though it caught fire. She'd never seen a naked man and would feel quite uncomfortable washing his private areas.

As if reading her thoughts, Rachel handed her a bowl to carry and said, "Perhaps Sam would deign to help you in this one instance. But afterwards, banish him from Brother Tobias's cabin or he'll be the next victim."

"Yes, of course." The last thing she wanted was for anyone else to catch the deadly disease.

As they made their way down the companionway, Moira recalled being exposed to a host of diseases and never once did she get sick. No doubt God had protected her and guard her health once more—of that, Moira had no doubt.

When they reentered Brother Tobias's cabin, Sam was gone. Bathing the sick man would be up to her alone. He lay beneath a single sheet covering the lower half of his body.

Moira stepped forward. The air in the cabin had grown thick and stale. Staring at the round porthole, Moira wondered if, perhaps, some fresh air would help the man's disposition. She made a mental note to inquire after she scrubbed up

Brother Tobias.

Rachel remained on the threshold. "Are you certain about this, Moira? You are putting yourself in grave danger."

Moira wasn't afraid. All she felt was that peace that God said would surpass all understanding. "I will be just fine. Thank you."

"Very well." Rachel's smile looked rueful. "You're an angel. An absolute angel."

Moira smiled. "Hardly, but thank you. Now you'd best go—for your own safety."

Rachel gave a nod that appeared reluctant in every way. However, Moira's mind was made up. She would care for Brother Tobias and, if miracles should abound, he'd recover from his ailment.

She shook the extra water off the scrub brush and began at Brother Tobias's head. "Tell me if the scrubbing hurts and I'll try to go gentler."

"Feels rather nice, missus. It's been a while since I've bathed. I apologize for that."

"No need. All I need you to do is concentrate on recovering." Moira worked her way down his neck and then saw clearly the rash hidden beneath Brother Tobias's thick, brown chest hair. *Its typhus for sure.*

Sadness fell over her, although she would continue to hang onto hope. Nothing was impossible for God. He spoke the world into existence. Curing a man's sickness was surely a simple task for the Almighty.

Sam returned and Moira informed him of the arrangement.

"Why you?" He set his hands on his narrow hips.

"Because I've the least to lose." She whispered the answer while glancing over at the sleeping man in the bunk. "The captain must not get ill, Rachel either, for Anthony's sake.

And you've got a mother and brother, not to mention important news to deliver, so I—"

"Moira, if there is one thing I despise in a woman, it's martyrdom."

She dropped her gaze and studied the toes of her boots so Sam wouldn't see how his words had cut her to her soul. "I prayed as my parents did, according to the sixth chapter in the Book of Isaiah." The words came to Moira and she met Sam's stare. "'I heard the voice of the Lord, saying, "Whom shall I send, and who will go for us?" Then said I, "Here am I; send me."'"

Suddenly she missed Mum and Papa so much tears flooded her eyes. "Tending this sick man is nothing compared to what my parents endured." She barely choked out the last word before turning away.

"All right, Moira." Sam turned her back around and wrapped her in his strong arms.

Moira felt sure and safe.

"Don't cry." He kissed her forehead. "I only have your best interest at heart. I don't want you to catch whatever he's got."

"I believe it is the typhus. He's got a rash on his chest."

Sam released her, and Moira instantly longed to be back in his embrace. She looked on as Sam inspected the rash. He shook his head.

"Doesn't look good, does it."

"Nay, it does not." Moira asked him to wash Brother Tobias's manly parts. While Sam obliged her, she stood on the only chair in the cabin and opened the porthole. She breathed in the fresh salty sea breeze.

"Moira, look at this."

She climbed down to find that Sam had rolled the sick man

onto his left side and exposed a back that was slashed this way and that. Pus oozed from the deeper cuts.

"Looks like a cat-o-nine tails had its way with his flesh," Sam said. "Could be why he's fevered, wouldn't you agree?"

"Yes, certainly. But what of the rash?"

"Rashes come and go. Could be anything."

Moira couldn't disagree. Some fevers produced rashes and the illnesses weren't necessarily fatal.

Sam leaned over the monk. "Tobias, who did this to you? Who beat you?"

"I cannot say. We in the monastery took turns beating each other last month. A ritual, you see, so we could..." He inhaled a lungful of air. "We wished to suffer as Christ did during Holy Week."

"You poor, misguided man." Moira set her hand on his arm. "Our Lord would not want you to suffer as He did. Have you not read, 'He was wounded for our transgressions, he was bruised for our iniquities; The chastisement for our peace was upon him, And by his stripes we are healed?'"

"I have not."

"Our Lord suffered so we do not have to face such terror."

"Too late now," Sam muttered with a wag of his head. Several sandy-brown locks slipped from their queue and Moira longed for a chance to touch him, to brush the hair back off his face. He met her stare. "Wash his back carefully. I'll fetch some bandages."

"Thank you." In Sam's absence, Moira coaxed Tobias into drinking the rum-laced water that Rachel prepared.

"Bless you, my dear lady," he murmured before drifting into unconscious bliss.

Moira took the opportunity to thoroughly clean the open sores. She realized it was the smell from his putrid back which had filled the room earlier. But the open window now took care of the matter.

The man whimpered softly just as Moira finished up and Sam returned. With his help, she bandaged Tobias's back. They dressed him in one of Captain Harney's nightshirts and covered him with the blanket.

"I'll sit with him a while."

Sam shook his head. "I'd rather you didn't."

"Then who should do it?"

The muscles in Sam's jaw appeared and Moira looked away. A wife shouldn't defy her husband, but they weren't really married in Sam's eyes.

However, they were in Moira's mind—that is, she'd meant her vows—and her heart said as much each time she looked at Sam.

"If you insist, I'll not nurse Brother Tobias."

He shrugged. "I suppose that now I'm convinced it's not typhus, I will allow it."

Moira hid a smile. He certainly spoke like a husband. "Thank you."

His gaze traveled the length of her body, sending a fiery heat into her cheeks. His eyes fixed on hers once more. "I'll bring you some supper in a while."

"I'd appreciate that, Sam."

He gave her what appeared to be an affectionate wink and then left the cabin. Moira pulled the chair up to Tobias's bed and pondered whether Sam had changed his mind about their marriage or if the playacting had simply gone to his head.

111

Chapter Thirteen

Three days and three nights.

On his back, stretched out on his pallet, Sam put his hands behind his head and stared at the shadows waltzing across the cabin's ceiling. A moist sea breeze wafted in through the opened porthole. Moira would surely wear herself to the bone if she didn't get some sleep soon. Why she felt compelled to sit at Tobias's bedside escaped Sam's comprehension. The man had a fever from self-inflicted wounds. Her constant presence made no difference. This was Tobias's fight, and Sam felt sure that the stocky fellow would beat the fever. He seemed to possess a hardy constitution. Besides, Moira herself had said that life and death lay in the palm of the Almighty.

The ship rocked and creaked, movements and sounds he'd grown all too familiar with these past weeks. But even concentrating on them didn't diminish thoughts of Moira.

So what really irritated him about her good deeds toward Tobias? Why should he care? He'd been struggling to find answers to those questions for hours now and greatly disliked the conclusion. He cared for Moira—cared for her more than he wanted to admit, more than he should. And he envied the dying man. Truth to tell, at least to himself, Sam coveted her undivided attention. Moira ought to be seeing to her husband's comfort!

Except Sam had made it clear that this marriage was as temporary as this voyage and, unlike Tobias, he wasn't sick and dying.

Sam groaned. *Nevertheless!*

He tossed off the worn blanket and jumped to his feet. Still in his trousers, his suspenders dangling at his hips, his shirt pulled out, he didn't bother with his appearance as he jerked open the cabin's door. With purposeful strides he crossed the saloon. The wooden floor felt smooth and cool against the bottoms of his bare feet. Sam raised his fist to knock when the door opened. Moira's sad and weary eyes met his gaze and he hated the purple half-moons beneath them. She was much too pretty to sport such a haggard look.

"You're exhausted. I insist you go to bed and get some sleep."

Her lips parted and he predicted a forthcoming protest.

"You'll be no good to Tobias or anyone else," he said before she could speak. "You must take care of yourself."

"Oh, Sam…" Her shoulders sagged and she began to weep.

"I didn't mean to sound so sharp, Moira." He pulled her into his arms. "I'm worried about you."

She felt so slight, so delicate, and she clung to him as if he were her bulwark. He allowed himself to revel in the feeling. Her breath warmed his shoulder and he felt each sob before they even erupted.

"Shh, Moira, don't cry." He rubbed his palm up and down her back. Seconds later, he inched back far enough to wipe her tears away with his thumbs. Her hair fell over the backs of his hands. "After a few hours of sleep things won't seem so bad."

"Sam…" She hiccupped. "He…he's dead."

"What?" Both sorrow and relief washed over him. "Are you sure?"

"Of course I'm sure."

Sam stepped around Moira and checked for himself.

"You doubt me?

"No, no…I'm just surprised." He tore his gaze from Tobias's body. "I honestly thought the man would beat his fever and survive."

"I prayed he would."

Sam heard the angst in her voice and closed the distance between them. Once more, he gathered her into his arms. "You did everything humanly possible."

"Did I?" She laid her head on his shoulder.

"Of course—you did that and more. You didn't leave the man's side the entire time he was ill."

"He has no people. He was an orphan, taken into a religious orphanage. That's why he always helped out with the children…he swore it was the typhus."

"Well, I still disagree. The man died from those infected wounds on his back."

Moira's head moved as if she nodded. "But the rash on his chest…"

"Fevers can produce rashes too."

"That's exactly what I thought and Rachel said." Moira lifted her head. "And here's another strange thing—"

Sam had trouble concentrating with her face so close to his. All he could think of was leaning forward just a sliver and kissing her delectably sweet mouth.

"Some orphans survived their illnesses. The way I understand it, the typhus is always fatal."

"Yes, that's what I heard of it also."

"Still, I didn't want Brother Tobias to feel abandoned, and after he lapsed into unconsciousness yesterday afternoon, I sensed he would die." She locked her arms around Sam's shoulder blades and it felt quite natural to rest his whiskered jaw against her silky hair. "I didn't want him to die alone." She sniffed. "I thought it could be me someday, dying alone, without any...family."

"Moira, don't ask me how I know this, but I do. You'll not be alone in your life." Was that a nail being hammered into the coffin of Sam's bachelorhood? So what if it were? Moira Kingsley was the least demanding woman he'd ever met, next to his mother, of course.

She began to cry again and Sam's heart crimped. "Come, let's put you to bed."

"What's going to happen to Brother Tobias now?"

Sam gave in to the half grin tugging at his lips. "Darling daisy, death is the most that can happen to any man."

"No, I don't mean that..."

Sam led her to their cabin.

"I'm referring to his burial." She paused in the saloon. "He will get a decent burial, won't he?"

"Of course."

"Will the crew toss his body overboard?"

"I wouldn't say they actually toss it. They more or less slide it down the gangway into the sea."

Moira moaned. "If that's ever me..."

"Stop that talk." With his arm now around her waist he glided her forward.

"Just make sure I'm really dead before they..." A little sob broke through. "Well, before they slide me into the water."

"Moira, you are far past exhausted. Park your thoughts on something pleasant." Sam pulled back the blanket and sat her down. After removing her leather booties, he lifted her ankles onto the bunk. "Lie down now and close your eyes."

She sank back onto the lumpy mattress then rolled to her side. Sam heard her softly crying. How did a man handle such a situation? Reasoning with her hadn't worked.

He blew out a breath and remembered back to what his father did. Surely Mama suffered with such emotions.

Hands on his hips, he stared at Moira. It came to him then. Papa always treated Mama like some cherished possession that he didn't want to break. Well, then, he'd do the same.

At least for tonight.

Sam stretched out on the bunk beside her, but on top of the blanket under which Moira lay. He touched her hair and rubbed her arm. Within moments he yawned. His eyelids grew heavy. Perhaps she felt as drowsy as he did.

Her crying ceased and her breathing evened. Good, she slept at last.

With his arm slung over her waist, he pulled her close just before giving in to the sleep that beckoned him.

Chapter Fourteen
••••ᎧᏜᏛᎯᏗ••••

With only a few hours of sleep behind her, Moira stood with Sam on her left side and Rachel, Anthony, and the rest of the crew at her right. Canvas sails rippled and clapped above as they caught the wind. Hot August sunshine beat down on the ship while a gray chopping sea surrounded it as far as the eye could see.

"We gather together today to lay to rest the remains of the man known to us as Brother Tobias."

Sailors readied to slide the religious man's body down the gangplank. Sam and the captain himself had wrapped and buttoned Tobias within a gray muslin sheath. They couldn't take a chance of rumors of a contagion circulating among the crew. The fever-produced rash on the dead man's chest was disconcerting. To let it be seen by sailors dressing Tobias's body might invite rumors which in turn would produce mutiny.

Then, again, it might not, as rashes weren't uncommon to those suffering with a fever. Either way, Captain Harney wasn't willing to take a chance.

Moira's knees felt like gelatin. She turned and hid her face in Sam's shoulder so she didn't have to watch the body enter the ocean. Why it bothered her so, she couldn't say. She knew God's Word stated that to be absent from the body was to be present with the Lord. The physical body was merely a shell beneath which lay a man or woman's soul. And Sam said it was purely exhaustion and the fear of drowning which plagued her. Once she'd slept well, the fear would subside.

Sam's arm held her about the waist and Moira suddenly felt as secure as a fence post despite the anxious rhythm of her heart keeping time with the bobbing ship.

"He longed to emulate the suffering and death of the Savior," Captain Harney continued, "and, thus, he succeeded, although not by crucifixion, of course. The beating he took sufficed."

The sounds of fabric rubbing against wood reached Moira's ears, followed by a *kerplunk* she wouldn't soon forget. Only when Captain Harney led the crew in the Lord's Prayer did she turn back around.

Sailors swept off their caps in reverence, and Moira attempted to concentrate on the spoken words of Scripture. Sam's steadying arm brought her a measure of comfort, but her mind's eye saw Brother Tobias sinking deeper into the water, lower, lower, into the depths...

She sucked in a breath and realized she'd been holding hers. Sam's hold around her waist tightened. Was she losing her ability to reason?

She squeezed her eyes closed. *Lord, help me.*

The service, such as it was, ended, and the sailors went about their business as usual. Suddenly it all seemed like a bad dream.

"The sun is hot today," Rachel remarked, shielding her dark eyes. "Moira, shall we spend time together in the saloon sewing? It's cool down below."

"I'm afraid I'm putting Moira back to bed." Sam's determined tone surprised her and she turned to stare at him. He'd become awfully bossy of late. She'd like to tell him so, but felt so...*tired.*

"Sam's right. I need some sleep."

"Of course." Rachel gave her a quick hug. "How thoughtless of me. I should have offered to relieve you and care for Brother Tobias one night."

"Nonsense. You've got a crew of men to feed." Moira smiled at Anthony, who watched the exchange with a spark of interest in his gaze. "Not to mention a growing boy."

"True enough."

Applying slight pressure on her elbow, Sam urged her steps forward. He said nothing more until they entered their cabin below deck.

"If you're not up by mid-afternoon, I'll awaken you. Otherwise you may not sleep tonight."

"Thank you."

He turned to go.

"Sam?"

He glanced over his shoulder, eyebrows raised expectantly.

Moira wetted her lips. "Brother Tobias said he was on his way to help missionaries in the state of South Carolina who have started a church and school in an Indian outpost."

Sam stepped back into the cabin and closed the door behind him. "Where in South Carolina?"

"Northwest of Charleston. Isn't that near where you hail from?"

"It is." Sam placed his hands on his hips. "Did he say what the outpost is called?"

"He didn't know, but I hoped you would. You see, I've

been thinking that perhaps I should take his place. After all, there are no such things as chance, luck, or coincidence in a believer's life. God used you to bring Brother Tobias aboard the *Seahawk* for a reason. Perhaps it was to lead me to these missionaries and help with their ministry to the…what did you call your mother's people? The First Nation?"

Sam nodded. "But I hardly think that outpost would be suitable for you. The cabins are made of hand-hewn wood. There are no papered walls. Just logs and clay."

"I've lived in more primitive homes."

Sam narrowed his gaze. "I think finding a good family for you, one with means who require a governess, would be more suitable."

"I think not." Moira looked away and moved toward the bunk. "Besides, my future is not your problem to solve. You've made that very clear. When we dock in Virginia you'll seek to annul our marriage." She chanced a glance in his direction. "All I need for you to do is point me in the right direction and I'll go from there—alone."

"What nonsense." Sam sent a look heavenward. "You'll not be happy, living in a rugged outpost. It's a tough life. One must scrape by, day after day, hunt for food, battle the elements, the rains, the floods, the freezing cold in winter and the extreme muggy heat in summer."

"You see it as scraping by, but I call that true living by God's hand. I was raised for such a life since birth."

"We'll discuss the matter further, after you've had some sleep."

Moira opened her mouth to reply, but Sam left the cabin so quickly she didn't get a chance. He closed the door behind him with more force than necessary.

Their conversation had, indeed, come to an end.

•••• ᏨᎮᏏᏋᏬ ••••

Sam found a comfortable spot on the deck and leaned back and watched the stars. They looked sharp against the backdrop of the inky sky. The sails of the *Seahawk* lay furled, but at the ready in case the wind should pick up. It seemed like an eternity since even a slight breeze had wafted over the vessel. At this rate, he'd never make it to Washington in time to warn President Madison of the British attack on the United States Capital.

But even that didn't seem as impending as the situation with Moira did.

Sam folded his arms. In the past eight days she'd kept her distance and occupied her days by helping Rachel in the galley and sewing. When Sam managed to catch up with her and attempted conversation, she replied with short answers that invited no further interaction. He should be pleased by that, shouldn't he? She'd taken his words to heart. He'd said he planned to annul their marriage, and that it was all playacting to cover lies which had worked to both their advantages—or so he thought. But lately his words came back, teasing, taunting, and haunting him. Though he justified his statements with logic, he couldn't help feeling that once the *Seahawk* dropped anchor he'd lose Moira forever.

Perhaps he'd already lost her.

Mayhap she'd never been his to lose in the first place, although he couldn't deny a certain spark between them right from the start. Her small shows of affection seemed to say she experienced the same feelings. It was as if they were meant to be together from the beginning of time. Sam and Moira. Moira and Sam.

Like divine affirmation, a star shot across the sky like a

silver bullet in the night. Quite a sight to behold.

A smile twitched his lips, until he remembered his duty to his country. Was it not to be first and foremost in his life? Did he not swear an oath to protect United States interests and learn British plots and foils, then bring back news to President Madison himself? Where could a wife fit into such a lifestyle—with such a duty? The president's men would call her a liability instead of an asset, of that Sam was sure.

Better to let Moira be. Forget her. Focus on his mission, as inconsequential as it seemed at this very moment.

Sam brought his fist down hard on a nearby wooden barrel. He'd gotten himself in quite the predicament. Duty, on one hand, to his country and, on the other, responsibility for Moira. After all, he couldn't simply allow her to go headlong into South Carolina, traveling alone and to a village where trappers and all manner of unkempt men stopped to trade with the Catawba. They filled their pockets with coins, only to spend them again at the small saloon and eatery, run by Sam's relatives. True, if the outpost Tobias spoke of proved to be the same village in which Sam grew up, his brother Asher and his wife would be there. Mama, also. They would look out for Moira's welfare.

That is, if Tobias's outpost and Yemassee Village proved to be one and the same, which was doubtful. There were many outposts located west of large cities, and they seemed to net all the riffraff between Virginia and Florida. Sam had seen his fair share come and go for years when he worked for his father's blacksmith shop and livery. Surely such a band of merry men, as in the days of Robin Hood, could use a good Christian sermon from time to time. The villagers would most likely have welcomed the missionaries as they brought with them a semblance of law and order.

But Sam had no plans to return home. Not now. Not ever. Certainly, he loved his brother and mother, but they wanted him to remain among them and take over his father's forge. Mama said it was "written in the stars." Still, Sam refused. He'd had bigger plans for himself. Plans to earn wealth. To live in luxury.

Thus far he'd succeeded.

And then he met Moira.

He churned out a low growl. Now he found it difficult to imagine his future without her.

Sam ceased his stargazing and cast aside his muse. There was time to figure out what to do. No decision needed to be made tonight. He stood and stretched and conceded a yawn.

"Time for bed, Mr. Stryker," the night watchman called from his perch high above.

"Aye, Mr. Abbott." Sam gave him a mock salute and heard the fellow chuckle.

A yearning for sleep weighed on him as he made his way down below and through the saloon. But when he tried to enter the cabin he still shared with Moira, to keep up appearances, of course, he found the door locked.

So the chit had locked him out. Fury burned his gut. He clenched his jaw. "Open up this door, Moira. Now!" He cared not if he awakened her, although it occurred to him on more than one occasion that he could find an empty bunk and sleep more comfortably in it than on the floor. Still, he'd never made the move. "Unlock the door. I'll not say it again."

"Nay, Sam, I cannot." Her soft voice sounded as if she stood right behind the door boards.

"Why in heaven's name can't you?" He placed one hand on his hip and the other on the doorframe.

"Sam…"

123

He tipped his head. Something wasn't right. He heard it in the weak lilt of her voice. "Moira, what's happening? Tell me."

"I have a headache, Sam." She seemed to choke on the words. "It came on late this afternoon."

"A headache?" He grunted. "Surely Rachel has some remedy for it."

"Yes, she gave me something, but it hasn't abated. It's gotten worse."

"Open the door." Sam would not stand here and banter such silliness. Why should a mere headache keep him awake tonight?

"Brother Tobias had a headache, Sam. Remember?"

Her words hit him like a fist to his midsection. Of course. Tobias had a headache for a couple of days and then the fever came on…

"Open the door, Moira."

"Nay, I do not wish for you to get sick."

"Too late for that, I'm afraid." A sort of peace settled over him and he believed he wouldn't get whatever sickness ailed her. One thing was sure, however, it wasn't the typhus. It couldn't be. Sam would never forgive himself for bringing that monk aboard if something happened to Moira. Surely God in His goodness wouldn't allow her to suffer, since she'd seen to the man's comfort until his death.

"Sam…"

Her voice trailed down the length of the door and then he heard a sound like Moira's head thumping against its bottom. "Unlock the door so I may help you."

No reply.

Had she fainted?

"Moira!"

Sam got down on his belly to peer beneath the uneven door boards and saw her lying in a heap, surrounded by her nightdress. Her unbound, sun-kissed brown hair fanned her head.

"Blast it all!" He got to his feet. He could hardly kick in the door with her lying directly behind it.

Kneading his jaw, he gave it a moment's thought before examining the knob and lock. He may be able to pick it with a hairpin.

"I'll be right back, my darling daisy." Would to God she could hear him. "You're going to be just fine."

Every nerve taut, he prayed it might be so as he dashed to the Harneys' quarters in search of Rachel.

Chapter Fifteen

Sam swabbed Moira's fevered brow. She'd slept relatively peacefully while suffering a headache. Rachel's herbs and an extra bit of rum in her water greatly helped. But then the fever came and the longer it lasted, the less her chances of survival.

It was going on five days now.

"Get well, Moira." Sam bent to place a kiss on her overly warm rosy cheek while sorrow pressed in on him. "I've been thinking about that first night we met. I've concluded that I never would have actually killed you." The grin that pricked one corner of his mouth felt both amused and sorrowful. "I've never killed anyone, save in self-defense." He lowered his voice. "But that's between us. After all, I've got a reputation to live up to."

He dipped the rag in the bowl of cool water and wrung it out, then swabbed Moira's hot skin just as Rachel instructed. He prayed the Almighty would heal her. Ironically, he hadn't communed with God since Pa's murder. And yet Pa, an honest man, dedicated father, and devout Christian had perished. Why did God allow such things? A good man died while his murderers walked free. How had it been fair and just?

Sam rummaged through his memories as he wiped down the skin on Moira's listless forearms. Pa had hammered his faith into both Asher and Sam just the way he hammered out horseshoes on his anvil. Faith made sense back then. Less so after Pa died. And the various religious courses that had been required while Sam posed as a student from the colonies only muddied the waters. What did Pa used to say? Knowledge puffed up a man's pride but wisdom came from God.

Now, however, when it came to Moira's life, he knew beyond all reason that it came down to God's will and that no amount of herbal remedies would override His divine decision.

But why would God listen to Sam's petitions? He didn't deserve to be heard in heaven.

Perspiration trickled down his temples and Sam wiped it away with his shirt sleeve. The cabin had become so stuffy in the late afternoon heat that he could barely breathe. But it was hotter outside. Worse, nary a breeze blew. At this snail's pace, they'd dock in Virginia by Christmastime!

Moira groaned and Sam shook off his thoughts.. "Moira, can you hear me? Open your eyes, darling daisy."

Her eyelids remained shut, though she rolled her head from side to side.

Sam tried to get her to quiet and drink some water. Amazingly, she drank, except Sam noticed her wince.

"What is it? Are you in pain?"

Many moments went by and Sam figured she wouldn't respond.

"My throat…" She croaked like a swamp frog, but Sam perked right up. "My throat is terribly sore."

Sam sat back, welcoming the sudden hope filling his insides. 'Twas good news; a sore throat was not a symptom of the typhus. "Rest easy, my love. You're going to be all right.

Hear me?"

Sam put the wet rag across her head once more and, again, he wished he weren't so powerless.

Rachel entered the cabin a while later, bringing Sam a tray of supper along with broth and water for Moira. "How is she?"

Sam tore his gaze from Moira. "She woke up long enough to take in some liquid and say her throat is sore."

Rachel's dark eyes widened and a little smile curled the corners of her lips. "Then it is not the typhus."

"I assume not." But Rachel's affirmation sent relief spiraling through him.

"Now if she could just rid herself of that fever..."

"Yes." Sam felt responsible for this calamity. He'd brought both the sickly monk and Moira aboard.

"You're doing a good job. Most men would leave the care of their wives to another woman or doctor." Rachel patted his shoulder. "Moira is young and strong and, unlike Brother Tobias, doesn't have a back full of infected gashes."

Sam looked up at Rachel in time to see her shudder at the memory.

She met his gaze. "You're a fine husband to her, Sam."

"She deserves finer, that's for sure."

"Nonsense. Now eat some supper to keep up your strength and see if you can coax her to take some broth."

"Your wish is my command, madam."

Rachel snorted a laugh and headed for the door.

After she'd gone, Sam leaned close to Moira. "Hear that, darling daisy? Rachel said I'm a fine husband." A shame that his wife might find it more a joke than a compliment.

When there was no response, Sam stood and stretched. He picked at his supper and lit a lamp after the sun sank behind the western horizon. He heard the slap of the sails and Harney shouting a string of commands. They were moving.

Sam unlatched the porthole and a cool wind struck him in the face. He breathed deeply of the fresh, salty night air then quickly closed the window so Moira wouldn't get chilled.

She stirred and he stepped over to her bedside. "Here, try to take another drink." With his assistance, she took several swallows of the broth then lay back against the damp bedding.

"Open the window again, please, that I may breathe in more fresh air."

"I'm not sure that would be in your best interest." He felt her forehead. Still much too warm. "You've still got a fever."

"On the contrary. I believe fresh air will do me much good."

"Well..." He didn't want to deny her such a simple pleasure, but he had an inkling it ran contrary to popular medical beliefs.

He thought of his mother. She'd tell him to open the window too.

A guffaw worked its way up and out his nostrils. Mama would like Miss Moira Kingsley...er, Mrs. Sam Stryker.

"Very well. I shall open it, but only for a minute or two."

Beneath the lamplight, gratitude shone in Moira's fever-bright eyes. True to his word, Sam opened the porthole again.

Activity above deck seemed to have increased and one glance toward the darkening horizon told him why. A ship. Was she friend or foe?

"Moira, I shall return shortly. I promise."

She gave a weak nod, and Sam took off to find out which ship approached them.

••••ᏩᏋᎩᏋᎧ••••

Standing on the main deck, Sam watched the other merchant

ship near until it bobbed starboard side and parallel with the *Seahawk*. The crew of the *Lady Magenta* was well-known to Harney and his men. Sam had breathed sheer relief when he learned that, like the crew of the *Seahawk*, they were United States merchantmen. But their news of Virginia's fate caused Sam's heart to sink like an anchor.

"The Brits burned the U.S. Capital," the captain of *Lady Magenta* hollered across the distance. "Then they took Alexandria and occupy it as we speak. We've heard they have set their sights on Baltimore now."

Sam hung his head back and squeezed his eyes closed.

"And what of President Madison?" Harney bellowed.

"Escaped along with the congressmen."

Relief spiraled through Sam. Thank God the president and statesmen ran the country, and not the Crown.

"No passage into Virginia," the other captain called. "We've set sail from Florida, but heard tell of British gunboats everywhere along the northeastern shores of the U.S., from Canada south to Virginia. My suggestion is to head for South Carolina. The British blockade doesn't extend that far south. Not yet, anyway."

The banter continued, but Sam felt heartsick. He traipsed to the hatch and returned to his cabin below deck. Moira had turned onto her side, but appeared to be sleeping.

"Blast it all!" Sam punched his fist into his palm. The very news he carried for President Madison was of no use now—now that the worst had happened.

He looked upward. *Why? Why, God, would you allow the U.S. to fall back into the hands of tyranny?*

The story of Jonah flashed through his mind. Jonah and the big fish that swallowed him whole because of his disobedience. In the belly of the beast, Jonah ruminated over his own will and God's. Once he surrendered to God's will, the big fish spit him out and he found himself in a land he didn't find worthy of his visit. He was surrounded by people who, Jonah determined, didn't deserve God's mercy and grace.

But God saw the circumstances differently.

"Sam?" Moira's gaze pinned him to the scuffed wooden floor and he recognized the concern in her eyes. "What's happening outside?"

"Nothing to fear, my darling." Sam put his hands on his hips. "But it appears the Almighty is pointing me toward home, whether I wish to go there or not."

Moira seemed to strain to keep her eyes open, but her dry, cracked lips worked a smile nonetheless. "Then you'll escort me to the missionaries at the outpost?"

Oh, how he wished she'd get that idea out of her head. "We'll discuss the particulars when you're better." He crossed the room and sat on the edge of the bunk.

She replied with a hint of a nod before succumbing to another deep sleep.

Chapter Sixteen

Nightfall brought the steady drumbeats that carried across the muddy river.

"No, Papa, don't leave me." Moira fought against the rushes that grew thicker and taller as she tried to reach her father. "Wait, Papa. Don't go!"

A snake's face, the size of a full-grown man's, rose up and blocked Moira's path. His laughter sounded like Uncle Tyrus's.

Moira screamed.

The river melded into the deep, deep ocean. Blue-green suddenly surrounded her as far as she could see. Nothing and no one to hang onto.

Lord, save me!

Despite her efforts to stay afloat, the water covered her face and the world blurred as she sank. She kicked and clawed, desperate to resurface, but the current dragged her down deeper, deeper...

"The Lord is my shepherd; I shall not want."

Her memorial—except she was still very much alive. She fought the rough sack that covered her as she lay on a hard plank as Brother Tobias had.

"He maketh me to lie down in green pastures: he leadeth me beside the still waters."

She knew to whom the voice belonged...

"Sam! Help me, Sam!" She tried to rip open the stitches sealing the sack. "Sam!"

She opened her eyes and sucked in a breath. Precious air. She gulped it in. "Don't throw me overboard," she panted. "I'm not dead yet."

"Shh...I'm here, darling." Sam held her trembling hand between both of his steady ones. A single flickering candle cut through the darkness around them.

"I was drowning." The words came out on breathless puffs. "I couldn't breathe."

"Just a bad dream."

"Nay. 'Twas real. I was about to slide down the plank, like Brother Tobias."

"Shh..." He pushed her hair from her face.

"You were reading my eulogy."

He smiled. "I was reading the Psalms to you. You've been restless tonight, calling out for your parents, so I found your Bible. I thought hearing the Scriptures might give you peace."

"Oh, Sam..." Moira still felt breathless. "I couldn't breathe." A sudden and violent coughing attack rocked her body, leaving her even more breathless than her nightmare. When she quieted, she wheezed and then guessed her illness. "Pneumonia?"

"It appears so, yes. But the fact that you're coughing is good news, according to Rachel. We've been hoping...no, praying...that you'd wake up and cough. Our prayers were just now answered."

As if on cue, another wave of coughing hit. This time it left her with a mouthful of foul-tasting phlegm and a chest that felt as though it were on fire.

Sam encouraged her to spit into an empty bowl. Next he urged her to drink. The water tasted like rum and something else, something bitter.

"What is this that I'm drinking?"

"In addition to rum to purify the water, Rachel added quinine to your portion. She says it will help to loosen the congestion in your chest." A smile inched its way across his handsome face. "I believe you're going to be all right."

"So I was dying?"

"We feared so this past week." He felt her forehead. "But now your fever's gone. Glory be to God. It's a true miracle."

"I've not heard you talk about praising God and miracles before." Moira's chest felt like a mule sat on it. She drank the rest of the water.

"I've been talking to God quite a bit lately. It appears I've behaved like the Prodigal Son." A little smile twitched the corners of his mouth. "After my father was killed, I went my own way and God decided to turn me around and take me home."

"Home?"

"To Yemassee Village in which I grew up."

"Do you think that's where Brother Tobias was truly headed?"

Sam's shoulders rose and fell. "I reckon we shall find out soon enough. We drop anchor in Charleston tomorrow morning."

Moira didn't find this welcome news. She attempted to sit up and succeeded only when Sam assisted her. "I must make myself presentable." Her head felt too heavy for her neck to hold. She leaned back against the wooden plank wall.

"Not so fast, my darling daisy."

"Stop calling me that, Sam." She turned away from the surprise on his face.

"'Tis an endearment is all."

Moira hated her weakened condition, hated that she needed him so much. "Endearments imply an intimacy between two people."

"And?"

"And you're annulling our marriage as soon as your feet touch down on land. Your affection is as real as...as my nightmare." She allowed her body to slide back down on the bunk, but rolled onto her side, her back to Sam.

"Moira..."

"No! Don't tell me how impractical my feelings for you are. I'm quite aware of it." Tears burst into her eyes, but she wouldn't let Sam see a single one. He'd warned her from the start. "I owe you my life. I'm eternally grateful for all you've done for me. But I also know that"—she swallowed a lump of emotion and forced a steadiness into her voice that she didn't feel—"you could never settle for a daisy when an entire flower garden lay at your disposal."

"Hmm...well, I must admit that accurately describes my frame of mind right up until the time I met you."

Moira's emotions triggered another fit of coughing and within minutes she lay helplessly weak against Sam's shoulder. He held her close.

"This voyage has changed me, Moira. I can't say when it happened precisely, but I know I'll be debarking the ship as a married man, devoted to my wife."

Was he joking? Moira pushed off his shoulder and peered into his face. He brushed her tears off her cheeks.

"I don't understand."

"It's difficult to explain. First I began to think of you as mine. My darling daisy. Then I began thinking in plural terms, no longer I and me, but us and we."

"How poetic."

"Yes, very."

A smile overruled her tears and Sam urged her back onto his shoulder.

"I love you, Moira. Perhaps I've loved you since the evening we met."

Moira pulled herself back and stared at his earnest expression. "You're not playacting, are you?"

A slight wag of his head loosened a rakish golden-brown lock that fell alongside his face. "I am as candid as I know how to be, a terrible thing for a spy to admit."

His words fueled another smile. "I shan't breathe a word of it."

"I trust you completely."

She cupped his face and felt his stubbly jaw against her palms. "I love you too, Sam. But you already know that."

"I had an inkling, although before you got sick your actions befuddled me."

It took only seconds for Moira to remember. "The more time I spent with you, the more I loved you. I knew your plans for after we anchored and disembark the ship. I didn't want to get hurt any more than I felt I already would." She ran her hands down his face, absorbing his every feature. Then she wrapped her arms around his thick neck and leaned in for a kiss.

"Ah…my darling daisy is no longer withering. 'Tis a good sign."

Moira's cheeks flamed at her own brazenness as if her fever had returned tenfold. "Can a wife kiss her husband that way?"

"Anytime she wants to…all day long, in fact."

She smiled as Sam laid her back down on the bunk. As he stood she grabbed his hand. "There is room for you alongside me."

"When you're feeling a little better, my love. You must save your strength. Tomorrow will be a very busy day."

Chapter Seventeen

Moira sank deeper into the fragrant bath water. Hotel Charleston had exceeded her expectations. The walls were solid and papered and there were men's and ladies' bathtub rooms at each end of the hallway. Businessmen from all over the world came and went through Charleston's port and frequented the hotel. Whenever they ventured downstairs for an evening dinner, she and Sam met cotton and tobacco brokers, and traders of every kind of consumer goods—including African slaves.

Images of the poor souls being carted through the streets in irons scampered across Moira's mind and despite the early September heat, she shuddered. Slave trading proved a despicable practice—and Sam agreed. He said one day his mother's people could be the enslaved ones, being that there were more greedy white men than there were Catawba.

The last of the afternoon sunshine streamed through the second-story window. Noise from the street below wafted in along with the fat, buzzing flies. Moira swatted one away, then worked the bubbles into her hair. Over the past two weeks as she recovered from pneumonia, she'd enjoyed an evening bath to cool herself from the heat of the day. But as she'd grown stronger, she'd grown bored. Bathing was the one activity Sam and the doctor allowed her.

Meanwhile, as she convalesced, Sam purchased supplies they'd need to set up housekeeping. He'd already sent a message to his brother and mother and learned his childhood home near the smithy/livery was vacant. The small village was still in need of a blacksmith. So, after purchasing a wagon and a team of mules, a horse, and sundry other supplies, he began buying new, practical gowns for Moira along with newspapers and other publications to help pass the time. Each day Moira felt more anxious to begin her new life at the outpost.

A smile twitched her lips. So now that the doctor had pronounced her well enough to travel, Sam advised her to enjoy one last luxurious bath, for it may be the last she'd get for a long while. Tomorrow morning they'd pack their wagon, hitch up the horses, and head for the outpost.

Rinsing her hair, Moira finished up and stepped from the brass tub. The assistant, a large black woman named Harta, handed her a towel and led her to the dressing table.

"You all clean and cooled off now, Miss Moira." Harta took the hairbrush from Moira's recently purchased amenities and worked it through her long, straight hair. "I hears you be leavin' us on the morrow."

"Yes, that's right." Her insides fluttered with anticipation. Would Sam's mother like her? Would the missionaries accept her help? After all, she wasn't Brother Tobias, and now she was a married woman. Would they allow her to teach the village children? She stared down at her flat belly. Mayhap by the end of the year she'd be expecting a babe of her own.

"You be'n one o' da nicest British ladies I ever knowed. You ain't got your nose stuck up in the air."

Moira smiled. "Thank you, Harta. You're very nice yourself, you know."

"Well, I sure does try. I sure does." The woman peered over Moira's shoulder. "You want I should pin up yo' hair?"

"Yes. Thank you. We'll dine downstairs tonight." After tomorrow she'd not have pampering and luxury such as the likes this fine hotel offered.

Dressed again, her hair expertly pinned, Moira left the bathtub room and made her way down the hallway. The door of the room she shared with Sam stood open. Stepping inside, she saw Sam pacing the carpeted plank floor. She closed the door behind herself.

"Something amiss?"

"No." He looked up and smiled. "In fact, I've a grand surprise for you."

Moira glimpsed the slip of paper he held in one hand. "Oh?"

He strode toward her. "My brother and mother are downstairs, waiting for us in the dining room."

"Really?" Moira patted the back of her hair, glad she'd had Harta pin it up. She'd be sure to look her best tonight.

"They'll journey back to Yemassee Village with us in the morning."

"They traveled a long way for dinner."

"There is a reason for it."

Moira tipped her head. "What is it?"

"The missionaries are with them. They're excited to...to meet you. They couldn't wait."

"Then that means they're not terribly disappointed I'm not a man."

"They're not disappointed. In fact, if I didn't believe in miracles before, I do now." Sam cupped her face and placed a kiss on her lips. "Hurry and get dressed, my darling, and we'll go down for dinner. Wear the dress from your engagement party. I'm partial to it."

She blushed at his wink and set off to change clothes.

"Have you the token we discussed for my mother? Don't forget to bring it."

"I won't." Moira eyed the pink dress in her arms and recalled the gold bangle Aunt Aggie had allowed her to wear to that fateful engagement party. Aunt Aggie had thought it too plain for her tastes, but said it suited Moira perfectly. Plain. She willingly offered it up as the gift to present to Sam's mother. According to tradition, she would either accept or reject it—and Moira—into the Stryker family.

"Mama will like your gift very much."

"I hope so." She donned her gown. "And now I need your help." Moira turned her back to him. "Will you assist me?"

"Of course." Sam made quick work of fastening the tiny pink buttons. The original task belonged to the ladies' maids whom Aunt Aggie had hired.

"Finished." Taking her by the shoulders, Sam spun her around. "You look even more stunning than you did months ago when you first wore that dress."

"Oh, Sam…" Moira's cheeks bloomed like Aunt Aggie's rose garden. "The things you say."

His eyes darkened.

"Thank you." Moira was learning to accept his compliments without questioning whether she deserved them. Sam promised his words were not vain flattery. He meant them.

Sam shrugged into his dark-brown frockcoat. He'd dressed in a white shirt and cravat over which he wore a cream-colored waistcoat and breeches. On his feet were black boots that came almost to his knees.

"What a handsome couple we make." Sam kissed the curve of Moira's neck and her knees weakened.

"I am so much in love with you that it aches." Taking him by the lapels of his coat, she pulled him close, speaking close to his mouth. "A shame we can't beg off dinner and stay here together."

"Do not tempt me, woman!"

His theatrics made her giggle.

Smiling, he placed a kiss on her lips then offered his arm. Moira threaded her gloved hand around his elbow.

They made their way to the hotel's dining room on the first floor. Only a handful of patrons were scattered about the room at this early hour. A gentleman with dark hair, suntanned face, and dusty brown suit was the first to greet them.

He and Sam embraced and slapped each other on the back.

"Moira, this is my brother, Asher."

She gave him a polite curtsy. "Mr. Stryker."

He bowed. "But, please, you must call me Asher. You are my sister now."

"Very well...Asher."

He looked back at Sam. "You look no worse for wear, my brother."

"You look well also."

"I am." He smiled so broadly, Moira could practically count all his even, white teeth. "I will soon become a father. My wife, Nizhoni, is great with child."

"Congratulations!" Sam chuckled and put an arm around Asher. "I take it your wife stayed at the village."

"Yes. It is too close to her time."

Moira caught sight of the woman standing in the shadows. Sam's mother? She, too, had dark hair like Asher.

As Moira watched the other woman, she thought her demeanor bespoke of her discomfort at the waiting. Moira tugged on Sam's arm and indicated toward her likely mother-in-law.

"Mama!" Sam led Moira toward her, and the woman stepped from the shadows. "I'd like to introduce my wife, Moira."

The woman gave a nod.

Moira curtsyed. "I have a gift for you. I hope you will like it." She whispered up a prayer that it would be so.

The native woman examined the gold bracelet with a stoic expression and for several long moments Moira feared she'd think it the same plain thing that Aunt Aggie did. But then a smile split her face and she pushed the bracelet over her wrist.

"I accept your gift, my daughter." She kissed Moira on one cheek then the other. "You shall call me *Meda*. You have brought my son back to me, just as I predicted." She turned to Sam. "You chose your wife wisely."

Moira wanted to laugh. The circumstances which brought them together had nothing to do with "wise choices."

"Nay, Mama, 'twas God who brought Moira to me, and God who brought me home."

The older woman's dark eyes fixed on Moira. "Again, I thank you, my daughter."

Her words were salve on Moira's wounded heart. "It is I who thank you. I love Sam very much."

"I can see that what you say is true." The woman glanced over her shoulder. "But now it is time to meet the missionaries who came to us in the winter months. They, too, believed their daughter was lost, but learned she is alive."

"How wonderful for them." A slight twist of envy pinched Moira.

She followed Meda across the dining room to where a gray-haired man sat opposite a woman wearing a wide-brimmed hat. The man stood and Moira's legs turned to gelatin. If it weren't for Sam's arm around her waist that suddenly seemed to hold her up, she'd surely be a heap on the darkly-stained floor.

"Papa?" It couldn't be. He and Mum were dead. Weren't they?

Moira swung her gaze to Sam, who wore a broad smile. "Your grand surprise."

She could barely breathe.

Papa rushed forward and pulled Moira into a snug embrace. His familiar woodsy scent enveloped her, and she heard him weep. "You are a sight to behold." He gently pushed her back and peered into her face. "And how lovely you've grown over these many months."

Moira blinked. Her mouth went dry. Lovely? Papa thought she was...*lovely?*

The slender woman wearing the hat turned, and Moira glimpsed her partially disfigured face. *The fire.*

"Mum?" She ran to her. "Mum...oh, Mum!" A sob escaped as they embraced.

Mum wept softly against Moira's shoulder.

"I thought you and Papa both perished."

"We assumed the same thing about you," Mum said.

"But why didn't you come for me?" She stepped back and turned to Papa.

"I did return, but it was two days later. Your mother stayed behind at the hospital as she needed medical care." Sorrow filled his gaze. "I asked everyone, but no one had seen you or knew of your whereabouts. Before long, I needed to evacuate for fear of another uprising. Your mother spent many months in the hospital, and once she was well enough to travel, the Missions Board sent us to America."

"And what of you, Moira?" Mum asked. "Where have you been?"

"In England. The doctors said I was in shock. And I don't remember anything other than bits and pieces until finally came to my senses at Uncle Tyrus's home." She pulled back and extracted her hankie from her reticule.

"Tyrus?" A deep frown settled on Papa's brow. "But we contacted him. He didn't tell us you were there."

"He didn't tell me you were alive either." Moira pushed back her shoulders. "And he was about to marry me to a monster! Furthermore, Uncle Tyrus spent much of my inheritance with riotous living."

Papa's face reddened.

"But then Sam rescued me." Moira stretched out her hand and Sam stepped forward. "Papa, I want you to meet my husband."

"It's an honor, sir." He gave a polite bow.

"Likewise, sir."

The men shook hands.

Papa puffed out his chest a bit. "Moira's mother and I are well-acquainted with your family. We have prayed diligently for her 'prodigal son.'" Papa chuckled. "I never dreamed he was my son-in-law."

Sam grinned. "God does work in mysterious ways, does He not?"

Mum laughed softly despite the obvious tears of joy in her eyes.

Papa turned to Moira. "I will deal with my brother Tyrus."

"Don't bother, Papa. Sam helped me collect most of my inheritance before we left England. I'm sure Uncle Tyrus wasn't left with much if any money at all. Let that be his just desserts."

"Nay, daughter. The law ought to be involved."

"I would ask you to leave the matter alone, sir. At least for now." Sam placed his hand on the small of Moira's back and glanced around the room. "I, too, had a mission, and it would be best if we did not alert British authorities."

The storm in Papa's gaze dissipated. "Ah, yes, well...then we shall let it be for the time being."

Asher politely seated his mother at the table behind Mum and Papa.

"Shall we sit also?" Sam indicated the empty chairs around the same table.

He seated Mum first and then held a chair for Moira. When Sam sat down, Moira glanced at the faces around the table. She'd gone from feeling alone in the world to having a loving husband and now an entire family, complete with her own parents and a niece or nephew on the way.

God certainly had done exceeding, abundantly, and above all she'd asked or ever thought possible.

"To God be the glory!" Papa said exuberantly.

"Hear, hear!" Sam chuckled. Reaching beneath the table, he took hold of Moira's hand. She gave him a smile.

"Yes, indeed," she murmured. "To God be the glory!"

The End

Keep reading for a sneak peek at

BY

ANDREA BOESHAAR

CHAPTER ONE

"I've brought the remainder of the ledgers as you've requested madam, but I fail to see why a lady of your standing should have need of them."

"I'm sure you do." Lydia Easton fought off a scowl at Lester Walden as he deposited several books on her deceased husband's desk. She clenched her fists so tightly the tips of her fingernails dug into the soft flesh of her palm. "And you maintain that all of my husband's debts have been paid in full?" She sent what she hoped was a stern glance toward the balding accountant.

The rotund man puffed out his chest. "Why, yes. They are always paid on a timely manner."

"Good." She folded her arms and narrowed her gaze. "Then perhaps you'd like to tell me why this attorney—a Mr. Jesse Garnet—is suing me for such an exorbitant amount of money? Did my husband owe him the sum?"

"I'm not the one to ask for details, madam." Walden's voice dripped with condescension. "That would be Mr. Crubbs' department. He's your attorney."

"I'm well aware of his position and I've already sent for Mr. Crubbs." Lydia began to pace in front of her deceased husband's mammoth, mahogany desk. "Do you not understand that I cannot return to England until this matter is satisfied?"

"Yes, ma'am, but there's nothing I can do about it. As I said"—he spoke as if Lydia were a dull-witted child—"you must consult Mr. Crubbs."

"I will. You can be sure of it." *Another swindler.* "Very simply I needed to hear from your lips that my husband's debts have been paid and all accounting is up to date."

"They have and it is, Mrs. Easton."

She tried not to wince at the surname. She rued the day she married Orwell Easton. But Father believed it was a good match and all of Lydia's friends were happily married and raising families of their own. Spinsterhood lurked, so she accepted the marriage proposal.

Little did she know then the horrors that awaited her in the United States of America.

As if he'd commanded it from the grave, Lydia's gaze slid upward to Orwell's portrait. The oil on canvas hung above the mantle like a tribute to a great man. In fact, there were portraits of Orwell throughout the house. Some depicted the man with his favored hounds. Another with his prize race horse, the very animal Orwell shot and killed after the stallion failed to win the Milwaukee Derby.

Lydia often wondered why Orwell hadn't put a gun to her head.

She set her jaw and refocused on the portrait. She'd ordered all of Orwell's portraits burned, but obviously had forgotten this one.

She tasted bile. In this particular painting, Orwell sat in an upholstered armchair, his bookshelves in the background. His stormy countenance seemed to mask his contempt of her; Lydia knew the expression well. She closed her eyes, fighting back the memories which threatened to undo her resolve. Nearly seven months had passed since Orwell died which meant she was no longer a victim of his cruel reign.

No. Now Lydia was free. Free from the man's rants, beatings, and barbarous possessions of her body. It had taken her a good three months to get a grip on her emotions and stop fearing Orwell would somehow return from the dead. Of course, Mother would tell her to read God's Word, but Lydia could not. The words meant nothing. Where had her mother's God been when Orwell terrorized her? There was not protection like Daniel the prophet experienced in the lion's den. Unfortunately, Lydia was mauled by the animal who had been her husband.

She shuddered and turned away so the accountant wouldn't see her emotion. She had to keep herself together long enough to dismiss this despicable man.

Like the way she'd let go of the rest of Orwell's dishonest, rude, and insensitive household staff before hiring her own people.

It was long past the time for this accountant to go and Orwell's attorney was next on her list. Had she possessed the presence of mind before now, she would have discovered their theft sooner. Thousands of dollars had been skimmed from Orwell's accounts—accounts that now belonged to her. Moreover, certain valuables in the house had mysteriously disappeared.

For the latter, Lydia suspected the previous staff helped themselves to what was legally hers. How dare they steal from her! She deserved every cent of her inheritance after suffering two grueling years of marriage.

"Yes, Mr. Easton would have approved of my systematic accounting," Walden said. He stared up at Orwell's portrait. "He always did, you know."

Lydia cast a glance at Mr. Walden. She had been a fool to trust him and Mr. Crubbs, except she'd been so vulnerable after Orwell's death and Walden and Crubbs had seemed so...fatherly.

But they'd deceived her.

She pushed back her shoulders. "Your services are no longer required, sir. You are, as of this moment, no longer in my employ."

"What? You cannot dismiss me like you did Mr. Easton's household staff! Why, I've been his accountant for more than twenty years!" Walden sputtered like a dying locomotive. "Your husband retained me for life."

"Unfortunately for you"—and quite fortunately for her—"Orwell is dead. Furthermore, according to Wisconsin State Law, I have every right to employ or dismiss whomever I please."

More undiscernable bluster.

"Besides, it was my dowry that put my husband's figures in the black, was it not?"

"So what if it was?" Walden ground out. "Once he married you, the money belonged to him."

Lydia placed her hands on her hips. "You've been Orwell Easton's accountant for...for life, as you stated yourself."

"Yes, but—"

"Orwell was a liar and a cheat. A miscreant to the nth degree." The words came out with more venom than intended. Yet, they were true. "You, Mr. Walden, are equally as unjust and I want nothing more to do with you."

"Now, see here, Mrs. East—"

"If not for your sloppy, scheming bookkeeping, I doubt my estate would have a lawsuit threatening it, and I would be on my way back home to England." Lydia marched toward the accountant. Remarkably, the man cowered. "Get out of my house, you scoundrel. Now!"

The man fled the study, but paused in the black and white tiled entryway. He shook his pudgy forefinger at her. "You will regret this."

"I doubt it." Lydia caught sight of Fanny, her nosy but well-intentioned maid and gave her a nod. Fanny straightened to her full height of nearly six feet, smoothed the skirt of her black dress and straightened the white apron pinned to her bodice and tied around her slender waist.

"Allow me to show you the door, Mr. Walden."

"I know my way," the man groused.

"Very good, sir."

Lydia leaned against Orwell's sturdy desk and hugged herself. One down. One to go.

Fanny entered the darkly paneled study moments later. "You were magnificent, ma'am. You didn't let that man take advantage of your good graces."

"Thank you." It had actually gone better than expected. Lydia felt somewhat empowered—just the way she'd felt after dismissing Orwell's household help.

"Do you plan to dismiss Mr. Crubbs too?" A smile crept across Fanny's thin lips and tiny creases appeared at the corners of her eyes. "I can hardly wait for that."

Lydia arched a brow. She tolerated much from her hirelings, like her outspoken rotund cook who always seemed to have a thick wooden spoon in her right fist, the muttering butler whose age-lined features would surely crack if he smiled even a little, and the young, vivacious Fanny, with wits as sharp as her tongue. However, Lydia needed to reinforce the boundaries now again. Otherwise, her paid help would surely take advantage of her the way Orwell's staff had done.

A sigh escaped Lydia as she collapsed into one of the winged-back, upholstered chairs near the hearth. This world was filled with villains and she couldn't wait to return home to her father's country estate. When Father learned what manner of beast Orwell Easton had turned out to be, he'd regret ever making the match.

But why had her parents not returned her letters or telegrams?

Lydia's stomach knotted.

"Shall I watch for Mr. Crubbs, ma'am?" A sparkle entered Fanny's green eyes. "I'll be sure to send him right in."

"No, thank you. I would prefer that you finish with the upstairs cleaning and allow Mr. Stiles to do his job as my butler."

"Yes, ma'am." Obvious disappointment washed over the woman.

Lydia regretted her harsh tone. "I imagine my family may arrive any day and, of course, I'd like to present them with clean bedrooms."

"For company. Of course." Fanny perked up, inclined her head and left the study. The heels of her shoes clapped against the marble stairwell only moments later.

How Lydia wished she could call Fanny a friend. But circumstances as they were, Lydia could make no attachments here in Milwaukee. Orwell never allowed her to develop acquaintances, so she hadn't a single friend in this city. She'd been Orwell's "pet" and never left this house unaccompanied. His staff then reported back to him about every person Lydia spoke to, every shop she visited. As for correspondences Lydia had penned while married, they never made it out of the house without Orwell's approval first. Her pleas for Father to come and fetch her only enraged Orwell and resulted in severe beatings.

Lydia stood and strode to the lead paned windows and stared into the courtyard. Her former bedroom was on the adjacent side of the house, and almost daily, while Orwell lived, she had considered flinging herself from her second story chamber window to the brick pavement below. Her fear was that she would survive. And then what? She'd be at Orwell's mercy all the more. Just imagining what he might have done to her if she couldn't fight back brought up another taste of bile that was difficult to swallow back down.

The only good in her life occurred when her wretched husband allowed her weekly visits to the Milwaukee Public Library. Those outings had been her lifeline. Books were her escape. And in many ways they still were.

Stepping to Orwell's massive desk, Lydia fingered the borrowed law text. She had studied it. She knew she had rights as Orwell's widow—rights her soon-to-be former solicitor failed to mention.

A man cleared his throat, giving Lydia a start. For a fleeting moment she imagined Orwell standing at the entryway of his study. He would have pounded her senseless if he'd ever discovered her in his study. This room had been off limits while Orwell lived and breathed.

But those days were over

Gone.

Dead and buried with the horrid man. Now Lydia could begin to live again.

She willed her heart to cease its hammering, and fixed her gaze on Mr. Stiles' tall, lanky frame filling a third of the wide doorway.

"Mr. Frederick Crubbs to see you, madam."

"Ah, yes…" With her hand on the law book, Lydia couldn't help the grin that tugged at the corners of her mouth. "Please, send him in."

Connect with Andrea

····᠐᠍᠍····

Andrea Kuhn Boeshaar is a Wisconsin author of over 40 books with ONE MILLION COPIES SOLD! The three components in all of her stories are faith, family, and forever relationships. In addition to fiction, she guest blogs and writes devotionals & magazine articles with the hope of encouraging readers wherever they are in their spiritual journeys.

For a complete listing of her books and to sign up for her newsletter, visit: http://www.andreaboeshaar.com/

Follow her on Amazon.com
amazon.com/author/andreaboeshaar

Follow her on Twitter:
@AndreaBoeshaar

"Like" her on Facebook:
Andrea.Boeshaar

Follow her on BookBub:
www.bookbub.com/search?search=Andrea%20Boeshaar

Honest reviews are always appreciated!

Made in the USA
Lexington, KY
13 August 2018